The]

by

James Calemine

Snake~Nation~Press
Valdosta, Georgia 2020

Snake Nation Press, the only independent literary press in south Georgia, publishes *Snake Nation Review*, a book of poetry by a single author each year, and a book of fiction by a single author each year. Unsolicited submissions of fiction, essays, art, and poetry are welcome throughout the year but will not be returned unless a stamped, self-addressed envelope is included. We encourage simultaneous submissions.

Published by Snake Nation Press
110 West Force Street
Valdosta, Georgia 31601
Printed and bound in the United States of America.
Copyright © James Calemine 2020
Photography by James Calemine
All Rights Reserved
ISBN: 978-1-7346810-0-0

No part of this book may be reproduced in any form, except for the quotation of brief passages, or for non-profit educational use, without prior written permission from the copyright holder.

Table of Contents

Waycross	7
Mass Murder America	10
Tainted Water	13
Bessie	15
Matthew & Irma	17
Eclipse	20
Hazel's Cafe	25
Two Teachers	28
Cell Phone Addiction	30
Rich Boy	34
Road Rage	36
Farmer's Almanac	39
Ballad of the Evergreen	42
Tobacco Road	45
Mojo Bag	49
Baby Doll	51
Electric Blue	53
Rose Hill Cemetery	59
Flirting With Arson	62
The Crew	65
Blind Willie Mctell	78
Black Flag Manifesto	73
Ides of March	75
The Four Horsemen	82
Crossroads	84
Power Grid Blues	87
Dear Ella	89
The Grand Princess	90
UFOs Over the Okefenokee Swamp	93

This book is a work of fiction. Characters resembling any person living or dead is entirely coincidental.

"Things are not the way they used to be…"
— Bob Marley

"If the Bible is right/The world will explode…"
— Bob Dylan

"Every normal man must be tempted, at times, to spit on his hands, hoist the black flag and begin slitting throats."
— H.L. Mencken

Introduction

As I write this Introduction, the world operates under a state-of-emergency Covid-19 lockdown. We live in a dangerous new world filled with fearful days–creepy truths. Things felt weird enough before this plague of 2020 descended. Historic developments transpire every passing day now.

Just when I submitted the original manuscript to my publisher the outbreak delayed the projected publish date. I decided the deadly virus fit right into *The Road To Hell's* thematic vision of dark realities in 21st century America, and beyond.

My editor suggested a shorter fiction collection this time around compared to my other books. I agreed. As E.B. White once said, 'the reader is always in trouble.' The attention span of the average person is eight seconds. So, there's no wasted words. I also changed some photographs.

Everyone will see themselves in these tales. The stories serve as snapshots capturing mass shootings, hurricanes, social media addiction, power grids, corruption, gambling, criminal liars, toxic water, UFOs, the coronavirus and other eerie realities of modern America.

For the best results, this book should be read in one sitting–straight through–like riding a bullet train. Like there is no tomorrow. This might be the last book you read from cover to cover. A couple of the characters appear in different stories that tie together a cohesive streamline to the book, which begins in Waycross, Georgia, and ends about fifteen miles away in the Okefenokee Swamp.

Ghosts of Gram Parsons, Bessie Smith, Blind Willie McTell, the Allman Brothers Band and Robert Johnson even echo through these stories. The fiction vignettes retain their own morality. The truth proves even more dangerous these days. Telling the truth can make you feel like a bootlegger racing to the county line at midnight. The truth can get you blackballed, blacklisted or worse. Just look around…

Who knows what's coming? Have faith, there will be a light, but rest assured it will be something we've never witnessed. These pages provide a stark glimpse into the past, present, future and *The Road To Hell*…

James Calemine
April 2020

Waycross

"You ever consider you might be in over your head? It's not too late to quit."

"I need that hard drive."

"You want the hard drive. You don't need it. Deep, dark water you're wading into here."

"Are you going to uphold your end of the bargain?"

"Sure, Jack. I'll uphold my end of the bargain. I just want to give you fair warning. You'll be on your own."

"I understand."

"Ok. Park in front of the Ritz Theatre on Pendleton Street. Be there at three tomorrow afternoon."

The call disconnected.

Jack knew Waycross, Georgia. Ware County served as an athletic rival when he attended high school. In his late teens, he discovered the music of Gram Parsons who lived in Waycross for several years. Other notable natives include the actor Burt Reynolds, pool player Johnny Archer, restaurateur Bill Darden and actor Pernell Roberts.

The Okefenokee Swamp borders Waycross. The frozen "Bubba Burgers" originated near Waycross, but for the most part it's just another small town in Georgia. What makes Waycross different from almost every other small town in Georgia is the cancer rate.

For years, residents complained about toxic waste in the air, soil and water. In 2005, the EPA took emergency action to deal with wastewater and removed 350,000 gallons from the environs. In 1964, Atlanta Gas Light closed their Waycross facility. Waycross natives claim this property serves as a toxic "hotspot" as well as the Seven Out facility and the CSX Railyard. The Seven Out lost its permit in 2004, but continued receiving industrial wastewater until the owner abandoned the site at an undetermined time afterwards.

Numbers on the cases of cancer are on the rise in Waycross. Rare cancers here appear in mostly children. Residents of Waycross have demanded answers from "authorities" for decades. Some reported seeing "blue fluorescent chemicals coming out of the sidewalks and from under people's homes."

Waycrossians claim Tebeau Creek and the Satilla River suffer from poisonous water affecting people and ecological systems in Ware and surrounding counties. Waycross residents are calling this dilemma a "silent disaster". At one point, city officials blamed the cancer on tree sap and from people flushing medications down the toilet.

Several reputable Waycross residents who retain connections to powerful people in the state claim pressure exists "to keep a lid" on this matter.

The Ritz Theatre in Waycross was established around 1913. Jack loved the old brick buildings in downtown Waycross. Some of the buildings stood vacant, like the Lyric Theatre—a couple blocks away. At three pm, a black suburban parked next to his truck. Jack unlocked his truck doors, and the passenger climbed into the front seat. Jack smelled his passenger's aftershave and cracked his window to keep from becoming nauseated.

"If I were you, I wouldn't take this story to the *Atlanta Constitution* or the *New York Times*. The whole state and beyond will be on your trail the next day. And you're not a local."

"I do not plan to contact them."

"Good. Here's the hard drive that contains everything you need to blow the lid off the situation. Be careful, Jack. You're entering dangerous territory—literally. Lose my number. I'll find you."

"Thanks George."

George stepped out of Jack's truck. George climbed into his black suburban with tinted windows, and shut the door. For the first time, Jack felt worried. He watched the black suburban driving away. He called George before he lost sight of him. George answered,

"Change your mind?"

"No. I just want to let you know if something happens to me--it's not suicide. No matter what the news says."

"Jack..."

"Yes?"

"You won't have time to commit suicide. Get out of town or they'll feed you to the fucking alligators."

Mass Murder America

"Turn on the news…"
"What now?"
"Another mass shooting happened today."
"Of course, it's Halloween. I'll call you back."

Dangerous times dominate America. Mass shootings transpire with a frequency nobody can comprehend. In two years this madness has accelerated at an alarming rate. It's beyond politics. Yes, assault rifles shouldn't be available for the public to purchase. However, something in our social fabric is causing mentally ill individuals to kill innocent people in public. Maybe social media serves to blame, but it's hard to quantify.

It seemed to accelerate after October 1, 2017, when fifty-eight people were murdered at a country music festival in Las Vegas. The lone gunman theory circulated as the media narrative and the story disappeared. Some reports indicated footage existed of two shooters from the same floor at opposite ends of the Mandalay Bay Hotel, but that didn't stick. Some say all the concert goers phones were wiped clean of videos and pictures by federal authorities. A scent of conspiracy always lingers in the air now. Maybe because the truth has become a conspiracy?

Always horrific, chaotic scenes flash from the media's savage news reporting the tragic details. A month later, twenty-seven people lost their lives at a Texas church due to gun violence. In January of 2018, another school shooting transpired in Kentucky. The same month three people got shot at a Texas gas station before the shooter committed suicide.

On February 14, 2018, seventeen kids died at Parkland, Florida, high school. On March 9, five people died from gunshots in California at a veterans home. On April 22, four people's lives got cut short due to more gun violence in a Nashville Waffle House.

On May 18, 2018, ten kids were murdered at a Sante Fe school. From May 30-June 4, seven people died in a shooting spree in Scottsdale, Arizona. June 28 marked the day of the Capitol Gazette massacre where five people were gunned down in Annapolis, MD. On August 26, three people died from gunshots in Jacksonville, Florida, during a Madden Football competition.

Four people were killed on September 6 in Cincinnati at a loading dock. Two weeks later in Maryland, a person killed three of his co-workers before turning the gun on himself. On October 3, in Florence, South Carolina, two policemen died in a standoff. Eleven worshippers were murdered at a Pittsburgh synagogue on October 27.

In Tallahassee on November 2, three people died at a yoga studio. Five days later, in California, thirteen people died in a restaurant shooting. On November 11 at an Illinois bar a patron was murdered in the parking lot. November 19–a gunman killed four people at a Chicago hospital.

2019 brought no sanctuary.

On January 23, five people died at a Florida bank. Three days later, a 21-year old man killed five people including his parents in Louisiana. A disgruntled employee killed five co-workers in Aurora, Illinois, on February 15. There was another synagogue killing in California on April 27. Three days later, two people got shot and killed at the University of North Carolina at Charlotte.

Another school shooting left one dead in Colorado. Twelve people died on May 31 in Virginia Beach by a stranger's gunshots. At the Garlic Festival, in Gilroy, California, a shooting occurred on July 28.

On August 3, 2019, twenty-two people died at a Wal-Mart in El Paso. The next day, nine people lost their lives at a nightclub in Dayton, Ohio. The Dayton killer also murdered his sister. On August 31, in Odessa, Texas, seven died at the hands of a suspect exchanging gunfire with police. On Halloween, another five gunned down…

The numbers add up. None of these numbers include killings in gang-related shootings in, say, Baltimore or Chicago. Numbing facts. A new era of mass murder America dawns.

He turned off the television.

Tainted Water

"Man, it's like these people are drinking tainted water with some vicious LSD in it."

"Yeah, a world gone mad. Corporate media doesn't help. They want everyone to be scared, and living in fear. Look at TV commercials. The news..."

"Everything comes through the TV or the phone. The one percenters control everything–media, insurance, big money and the politicians. They spread fear and propaganda. Hell, Alexa will eavesdrop..."

"It's not looking good. And people don't know their history."

"The Chinese own us. They own our medicine. Our citizens hate each other worse than our enemies like Russian, Iran, North Korea or China."

"It will get worse."

"You bet. We agree on that one. It's just anger and hatred everywhere."

"And we have another presidential election next year. Everyone will lose their mind at some point."

"Yes, ghastly shit like we've never seen is going to transpire. Sinister winds are blowing these days."

"Yeah, something's coming. You know what they say, you never miss something until it's gone. People will miss America."

Bessie

Anna bought a framed black and white photograph for two dollars at Goodwill.

"It's so sad. Can you believe a loved one sold her picture? So, I bought it. She's gonna sit on our kitchen counter."

He inspected the eight by ten photograph as he put on his seatbelt. Anna started the car, and he said in a levity-laced voice:

"She looks like the old blues singer Bessie Smith."

"Then let's call her Bessie."

"Alright."

Bessie leaned on a white rail that matched her gloves, the flowers behind her dress, purse and shoes. Her eyes appeared half-closed perhaps because of the sun shining in her face. Her smile emitted a warm glow--as a mother, daughter, sister and friend.

No notes, names or dates were written on the back of the photo. She looked around thirty eight years of age, but it was hard to tell. How old was she? When and where was this picture taken? When did she die? How? The picture contained a mysterious positivity.

How far did this photograph travel to end up at the Goodwill in Charleston, South Carolina, and now in his kitchen?

The next day, he poured himself a cup of coffee. As he chewed a bagel, he noticed Bessie's soulful, smiling face. He couldn't help but grin back at her picture in the frame.

Matthew & Irma

Once you witness twenty feet of high water and severe flooding you won't forget it. Such a sight alters brain chemistry. It transforms your perspective–especially when water rises around your town, business, street or home. High water makes you feel like you're living a scene out of the Old Testament. Much less, the disturbing news footage from devastated areas in Florida raises concern as the storm moves towards your coastal town. The rising tides send an ominous warning.

Nothing remained the same for our family after Hurricane Irma blew by our coastal home in September of 2017. The year before, Hurricane Matthew slammed a three hundred-year old oak tree into my parents' house. In retrospect, Matthew served as a warning. Irma brought the undeniable psychic damage the following year. We counted as evacuees for ten days during hurricane Irma. The thirteen barrier islands of the Georgia coast sat straight in the middle of both storm's paths.

If you grow up on the coast, you become accustomed to hurricanes. In recent years, they've been coming hard and fast. I remember watching scenes from Katrina in New Orleans during 2006. I always felt empathy for those storm victims living on the coast because it could just as well be us.

Right before Matthew, a hurricane hit Texas and I remember seeing people wade through chest-deep dirty brown water in their hometown with nothing but what was on their backs. Horrific scenes. Snakes slithered through the filthy water along with alligators, rats and debris while men, women and children looked for dry land. Some families stood trapped on their roofs.

Matthew arrived on the Georgia coast in September of 2016 in the middle of a contentious presidential race. Madness pervaded the air. The Weather Channel intensified fear and warnings for everyone in Matthew's path. Disaster proves to be great for television ratings. Since we resided on an island, mandatory evacuations were set into place. If children or elderly parents weren't involved, I wouldn't have evacuated for either hurricane. We drove to Atlanta to avoid Matthew.

We didn't know how long it would be before we could return home. Would we have a home to return to? I left my wife and daughters at the hotel and walked across the street to sit in a bar that first night in September 2016 of evacuation, drinking a margarita, to clear my head. I scanned my phone searching for any local news on the progress of the storm, but Facebook only revealed people talking about politics–not the storm threatening their friends, family and neighbors on the coast.

Their humanitarian Facebook platitudes did not correlate with posting about going to help place bags of sand near their friend's home only a few hours away. They only blathered about politics while safe at home. I knew then a dark era began to manifest. It pissed me off. Talking politics became much more important than helping people in the face of an act of God.

It felt like all levels of my life and the world–on a personal, professional and global sense–shifted. After four days or so they allowed us back onto the island after Matthew. Two days earlier, a friend who didn't evacuate the island texted me a picture of a three hundred year old oak tree that crushed my parents' garage. The clean-up took all year.

When a semblance of normalcy returned, Irma arrived in September 2017.

In the summer of 2017, my father underwent hernia surgery and endured a procedure to have several cancerous spots removed from his forehead. He beat lung cancer a few years back, and volunteered to undergo hernia and skin surgery. Yet, he'd not completely healed when Irma approached. Matthew remained fresh in everyone's mind from the year before as the Gulf hurricane Harvey tore through Texas.

We were next. Irma, a massive storm, gradually moved up the Florida coast. It pounded everything in its path. It looked bad. Everyone's anxiety returned. Fear. A storm of such magnitude makes sleep difficult. But, life elsewhere goes on. Business as usual. Time only stops for your community, not the entire world.

Again, no one wanted to evacuate but for Irma my parents evacuated to a friend's house in Atlanta, and Anna and I drove to Statesboro with our teenage daughters. Important business plans of mine were cancelled due to Irma, which affected the year's income.

When you must evacuate your town–for a wildfire or hurrican–matters boil down to a few essentials such as health. What to pack? What to leave behind? It brings intense stress. Storms lurk beyond your control. You're leaving your life behind far as you know. Long evacuation lines, empty grocery stores, booked hotels, gas shortages and spending money you can't afford are only the initial problems. Whatever you don't take with you–you may never see again. It's a rare perspective to operate under for–in our case–ten days.

TV anchors reported the storm with weird gleams in their eyes. Bad news always travels fast. Another mandatory evacuation was imposed on our community. More images of rising water and flooding streets circulated in social media.

After Irma, a shift in our lives occurred. We were allowed back on the island about ten days later. Overall, our island suffered only minor damage. We suffered less property damage than Matthew, but Irma's psychological damage proved definitive. My father's operations, evacuation and stress from Irma only weakened him, and ultimately his condition deteriorated. He died five months later.

Eclipse

The one-story brick motel, built in the 1950s, stood on the outskirts of St. Augustine, Florida. The motel was painted white with gold numbers nailed on every green door above the peephole. Green and white served as the motel's theme colors.

The room smelled like cigarette smoke. Yet, signs read 'No Smoking' in various spots around the room. One chair, one small table, a TV, two lamps, a Queen-sized bed, a wall AC and a small refrigerator furnished the grass green-colored room. The mirror showed streaks from a cheap cleaning product.

William, a forty-six year old photographer, sat on a plastic chair outside the room. His beard began to gray, his hair started thinning, but he still retained a body of great leverage. He wore a flannel shirt, faded blue Levis and no shoes.

Elizabeth, a thirty-eight year old art director, sat in the chair next to William. Her tight blue sweater revealed her hypnotic female anatomy as did her tight blue jeans. She was also barefooted. Elizabeth looked at William with her pale blue eyes and smiled. Her wavy blonde hair fell below her shoulders. Her smile emitted a soothing quality. She said to William,

"Well, here we are in room 357 at the Salt Air Motel for a rare supermoon eclipse."

"Yep. The first one in thirty years–September 27 and 28. They call it the Blood Moon."

"The snowbirds haven't arrived. This will be a good weekend to be here. The place is almost vacant."

"I'm glad we're here together, baby."

"Me too. If nothing else, you'll be able to take some good photographs."

"We'll see."

"Don't be negative, baby."

"I'm not being negative, Liz. It's realistic. We'll see if I shoot any."

"Kiss me you fool."

William leaned over and kissed her on the lips. Then Elizabeth said,

"I love you."

"I love you too. So, here we are at the end of time."

"Waiting on the world to end."

They laughed. William sipped his can of Coors, and mentioned:

"There's no doubt these are creepy times–things are going to get weirder. There's no time to waste. We have a Presidential race coming, a Pope visit, our girls are teenagers, ISIS, China, Russian, bills, refugees, school shootings and all the world's malice."

"Well, let's try to have a nice getaway baby. Let's enjoy the view."

The Atlantic Ocean conjured a cool breeze. Overcast skies loomed. A light fog floated in the air. The seabreeze felt thick. Elizabeth looked at her watch that displayed 6:32 PM. Friday. She lit a cigarette and said:

"I like this place. It feels like we're in a time machine."

"Yeah, either 1952 or 2052."

Elizabeth handed William the lighter, and he lit a cigarette. He took another sip of beer. He exhaled and mentioned:

"I've tried to do everything right and live my life on the square."

"When we get through all of this will you run away with me?"

"Absolutely."

They smoked in silence until their cigarettes burned down. William fetched two more beers. He sat back down and tried to explain what he was really thinking.

"I've got to generate more money–ASAP–or it won't be good for my health. Jessica lives in Pensacola and you know I only see her every couple of months, and it's painful. It hurts to be in this financial position. Obviously, I've been more concerned with Art, Ideas, Love–whatever, more than Money. These are venomous times."

"I know baby. I know seeing Jessica every few months is very hard. I can't imagine it. Things will change. We all need you. I need you. Jessica needs you. Even Sadie. She's around us more than her own father. Things will get better."

"Change is in the air. It's palpable." William paused, took a drag off his cigarette and mumbled,

"I think these clouds will spoil the eclipse."

"Remember our first night on the beach?"

"How could I forget? It altered the course of my life."

"I've been looking for you all my life."

"I'm a lucky man."

"I'm a lucky gal."

They held hands and looked out towards the dark Atlantic. William lit another cigarette, sipped his beer. Then he spoke:

"I wish I earned more money."

"Will, I love you more than any man I've ever known."

"I love you the same way."

"I believe in you."

"Thank you. I believe in you too."

"We've got to get your pictures in front of more people.

"I feel like I'm starting over again."

"You should hold back some photos."

"Those motherfuckers don't have one original bone in their bodies. And I gotta get another book out. These locals want me to take their picture, pay for overpriced food and drinks in their restaurants and bars, listen to their third-rate music, but they can't break with twenty dollars to buy a print? Fuck them. And they always preach: support the locals! Then they go out, follow me around and imitate my shots. And they think they're artists."

"You're a real artist–they resent it. You threaten their mediocrity."

They looked at each other and William whispered:

"You have the prettiest blue eyes."

"They're not as pretty as yours."

They kissed again. The salt air thickened. Waves splashed on the shore revealing a high tide. A rhythmic wash created a nocturnal mantra amid the deep south humidity. A magnificent silence between them caused a simultaneous glance. They both smiled.

The old motel retained a ghost-like quality. Weird old Florida. A ragged bygone glory surrounded them. William loved the motel sign out front, which served as the fulcrum for why they chose to stay at the Salt Air Motel. He believed a picture of that sign was worth the trip. He photographed it upon arrival today, and planned on getting a night shot–eclipse or not.

"All this worry has my nerves shot out."

"It's strange how we're both at the lowest ebb of our lives since we've been together."

He kissed her on the forehead, and stood up to say:

"I'm going to take a picture of that sign again."

"Let me get my sandals and I'll go with you."

They walked out to the motel sign in the parking lot. William snapped about twenty shots from different angles. He lit a cigarette and said:

"I love this place."

"We could just move in."

"A residency of sorts…"

"Make some friends."

"Meet new neighbors."

They returned to their room. William reached for two more beers. Elizabeth removed her sandals. Clouds obscured the moon. The eclipse counted as three hours away. Elizabeth asked William:

"Is there anything you want to do?"

"You mean besides get in your pants? Not really. Just look at the shots I took on the way down."

"Don't worry. I didn't bring you down here for nothing."

Elizabeth turned on the TV. William inspected his recent photographs on his laptop.

"Let's go for a walk."

"Okay. Are you taking your camera?"

"Yes."

They walked out in front of the motel. They gazed skyward. The sky appeared bright, but the Blood Moon remained obscured by thick clouds. William snapped a couple of photos he knew would never be seen like a songwriter discarding songs.

When they approached the edge of the sidewalk, Elizabeth asked:

"Do you think we can walk to the convenience store?"

"That's at least a mile."

"Then let's drive. I need some water."

Upon returning to the room, William wondered how the eclipse affected people. If the full moon could make tides rise–who knew what it could do to people? They stood at a crossroads and now was the time to make a life-altering decision.

Elizabeth smoked on the balcony, looking at her phone. He walked outside, and lit a cigarette. It seemed she read his mind.

"We will get through this strange time."

"I know we will, baby."

He leaned over and kissed her. William made his decision right there. He lit a cigarette. He looked for the moon. Time brought them together.

"Well baby, everything is okay. I love you," he said and embraced her.

"I feel exactly the same. Even though we're gonna miss the damn eclipse. Let me take you inside room 357."

Hazel's Cafe

"I need a definitive photo. I've taken hundreds down here, but I don't think I've captured THE ONE yet. I gotta catch a flight out of Jacksonville for New York tonight at 8. Do you know any good spots?"

"I've got a place."

"Where?"

"Hazel's Cafe."

"Is it on St. Simons?"

"Oh yeah. It's off Demere Road. It's on the left before you get to the elementary school. It's a wooden shack that was built around 1947. It's a photogenic power spot. Your city slicker editors will love it."

"I'm leaving the hotel now. I'll be at your place in ten minutes. I'll follow you there. Then I'll leave for the airport."

Ray followed me to Hazel's in his white rental Subaru SUV. I parked across the street and indicated for him to do the same so no cars would be in the shots. A light breeze swept across the island.

"Holy shit," Ray said, climbing out of his SUV with his Nikon D5 already pointing at the old juke joint. "Look at that old rusted tin roof!"

Ray began snapping photos–adjusting his lens.

"I love the vintage Coca-Cola sign that says 'Hazel's Cafe' over it. Just classic. I always loved this funky old place."

"You said it was built in 1947?"

"Maybe a year or two before then. It was an African-American eatery. In those days, there was Wilma's Theater, a place called The Pavilion and an old motel near where the school is now. Before our time."

"Unreal. This is all the original wood. It's so weather-beaten, rustic and just beautiful. Talk about hand-crafted. What's the story with this place?"

"Far as I know Thomas and Hazel Floyd owned it. It's been closed for about forty years. But it was popular back in the day where they dished out fresh local fish, shrimp, crab and even cooked barbecue in a pit around here somewhere."

"It looks like someone keeps it up," Ray said peering into the windows.

"And these palmettos have been planted within the year."

"The church just down this street, Emmanuel Baptist Church was built around 1890, I think. You might want a photo of that too."

"How is Hazel's still standing amid all this high-dollar island real estate?"

"Someone bought it back in the early 1990s for preservation, and they ain't selling it. I think the owner lives in that house back there."

"Damn, I would've loved to visit this place when they were serving food and drinks."

"Yeah, me too. But it makes a hell of a photograph doesn't it?"
The cotton-shaped clouds lingered in the early March sky that obscured the sun somewhat this afternoon. The light proved perfect.

"Absolutely. You've turned me on to a coastal treasure. This is one of my favorite subjects from my whole trip. I owe you one."

Six months later, Ray's coastal photography collection won a Sony World Photography Award that allowed him to show his work at London's Somerset House.

He never sent a thank you email, text, call or card.

Two Teachers

"All these kids know about life is what they learn through their cell phones."

"That's the truth. Cell phones have ruined the younger generation's mind."

"They don't know how to talk to each other. They fear nothing. They respect nothing. But a lot of what they experience isn't real."

"Their entire world is on a screen. All they ask is 'Can we play music on our phones?' or 'Can I go to the bathroom'?."

"We're old enough to remember life without the internet or cell phones--when you actually had to have some social skills. I bought my first 'bag phone' in 1993. It looked like a suitcase."

"This is the future of America."

"We're screwed."

"I feel sorry for them."

"Yeah, they have no idea how hard things are going to get for them."

"On the other hand, some of these kids are downright dangerous."

"For sure they're dangerous. The could make up some crazy fucking story and your life is ruined."

"It's happened before."

Cell Phone Addiction

Rachel scrolled through her Facebook page at work. She looked around the room full of cubicles and noticed several other co-workers hunched over their cell phones. A scent of fresh cheesesteak sandwiches, breadsticks and pizza drifted into the office from the break room where her company ordered food today since Christmas approached.

She noticed Veronica Wallace taking pictures of the company lunch spread and moments later she posted it on Facebook. Rachel didn't want to 'like' Veronica's post. Veronica loved posting photographs of herself on social media.

It dawned on Rachel how social media influenced people in strange ways. Most volunteered more information than people wanted. And everyone is so pleased with themselves. From her own experience–family, friends and lovers sought extreme refuge in their cell phones. She understood everyone is always distracted–even hypnotized–by their phones in this modern day and age. It's a way to avoid human interaction, but digitally stay in touch. People project images in ways they want their life to appear.

She believed too much social media causes mental disease–especially in young people. Rachel wondered how many relationships were ruined by social media outlets. The spying. The lying. The desire for 'likes' from suspected, potential or previous lovers. She knew–as did most of the office–Wallace participated in at least two affairs with co-workers that went unnoticed, or kept secret, from Mr. Wallace. One affair came three months after her husband's father died. Her husband's grief annoyed her. Yet, Veronica Wallace always justified her emotional distance from him. Even Veronica's friends kept her affairs secret from her husband. Poor bastard.

Rachel realized many of her friends based their self-worth on their 'selfies' and flirtatious attire to attract men. She knew many of her married girlfriends possessed a proclivity to post sexy selfies to attract 'likes' of the opposite sex because they craved attention from all the men–not just their husbands. They become addicted to the attention even from their female friends. None of these people existed as the image they projected of themselves.

Whatever flashes on the cell phone screen outweighs the person sitting next to you. They'd rather post on social media than respond to your text message, call or even talk to you in their precense. They desired 'likes'.

They wanted attention. Immediate gratification. Families sitting around their homes together, not paying attention to one another but texting or sifting through their various feeds.

No matter how tumultuous life could be, people continued taking selfies to obtain 'likes' because somehow that's more validation than they could get in everyday reality.

Rachel thought of Marie Rogers who one day needs prayers for her dim-witted sister going through another cheap drama or mind-bending crisis of profound inconsequence to her hypocritical religious advice.

The next day it's selfies on the beach in a bikini showing off her rack with her girlfriends as if life is beautiful. It's no mystery Marie Rogers never posted photographs of her husband on Facebook. She paid little attention to her husband unless it made her look good or worked to her benefit in the eyes of her digital friends or co-workers. Rachel wondered, which is it, do they need prayers–or just 'likes'?

Rachel understood even she–like most–suffered from separation anxiety if she weren't around her phone at all times. Her kids could send messages to friends that disappeared on Snapchat. These apps made secret relationships undetectable, temptation real and easier to hide.

The cell phone cost her at least one relationship. The food smelled delicious. She dropped the phone in her purse, and walked into the breakroom to eat a slice of pizza.

Rich Boy

I knew Billy Smith through various acquaintances in my hometown. His parents were a wealthy lumber clan from a neighboring county, and Billy moved to town about the same year I moved back from Nashville. Billy was not a self-made man.

As you know, rich people, especially those born with a silver spoon in their mouth, possess an inflated sense of themselves and their opinions. They proclaim to be experts in damn near any subject–especially music. I met Billy a few times. He appeared overweight with thick dark hair combed back with gel, and he wore the latest stylish men's clothes. He loved penny loafers. He really never earned a dollar on his own–his father's fortune made his life easy.

He fancied himself a ladies man as well as a photographer even though he didn't own a camera. He informed me he was a big fan of the Silvertones and other semi-successful bands that I recorded or played with over the years. He seemed genuine on social media, but then so does everyone. He also fancied himself a comedian. Billy told me he bought my last two albums, which my record label never informed me of and they keep accurate sales lists. So, he lied to me.

During Hurricane Matthew, Billy decided he'd ignore a mandatory evacuation, like many others, and remain in town. He informed everyone he would keep them posted on Facebook about how the storm was affecting our north Florida community in "real time". He offered to ride by anyone's house to assess damage, if any.

We were visiting my wife's family in California. So, a couple of days after the worst of the storm hit our small coastal town I contacted Billy and asked if he would drive by my home studio and ascertain if there was any flood damage.

"No problem", he texted me. An hour later he sent: "You're good".

Three hours later, my drummer called to inform me my studio garage was flooded and most of my vintage equipment--guitars, amps, microphones, drums, rugs and pedal boards–appeared ruined. Thanks for not driving by Billy, I thought.

The following fall, I received a call from Billy. I did not answer. He left a drunken message:

"Hey Ed! This is Billy. I'm up in Manhattan, and I was wondering if you could put me on the VIP list for this Silvertones show tonight. Thanks man."

Oh sure, you spoiled rich brat. Let me call up, my friends, this famous band, and vouch for you so you can go backstage and make an ass of me and yourself after you've lied to me twice. Fuck you.

Several weeks before this unsolicited call, Billy snuck backstage at a Log Cabin Pickers in Jacksonville, and when questioned what he was doing backstage, Billy told the band we were close friends. This was a band I traveled on the road with for years and I'm quite sure I never mentioned this rich boy's name. Billy fancied himself as a local celebrity of sorts on social media since he could afford to travel wherever he wanted on Daddy's dime.

The last time I saw Billy was at a street party for a Super Bowl outing at a local bar. He looked drunk. His powder blue-colored sweater was tied across his shoulders, his penny loafers shined with a new 2019 penny in each Italian loafer as he held a bourbon & coke in his left hand. Billy was one of those people that when intoxicated, they invaded your space by getting real close to your face when they talked to you. So close his sour breath made me want to wretch.

"Man I wish you had your albums on you, I'd buy them. But it's raining and I wouldn't want to carry them around and get them wet. I'll buy them from you next week."

I wanted to say, but you lied and said you already bought them. Then he began telling me how he snuck backstage at a Blue Sky show two weeks ago and how he walked in on the lead singer smoking a joint. I couldn't listen to him anymore. I noticed my wife was walking from the car and I started moving in her direction as he kept talking and I said,

"See you around."

No wonder folks hate rich people.

Road Rage

Cantrell minded his own business, stared out his open window while waiting for the light to turn green when he felt the car behind him nudge his 68 El Camino. Cantrell noticed in his rearview mirror, a young Caucasion man wearing a baseball hat backwards, gesturing with his left hand, as if to say, "Hurry up. Pay attention". Cantrell noticed the punk drove a Viper. The bumpers barely touched.

Near an old underpass, amid urban congestion, traffic flow stalled, and tensions heightened. The stoplight was red. Cantrell paid attention to the light. No reason existed for this kid to act in such an aggressive manner. Traffic allowed no movement. Cantrell could not fathom the nerve of this young driver, who risked damage to both vehicles only to antagonize with a slight vehicular nudge.

Cantrell wondered if his El Camino suffered any damage. For a moment he distilled what transpired, as if the kid's action was something too absurd to react to, or perhaps, too rude not to react.

The July heat stifled any breeze. Dead air beneath the underpass proved stifling. For the second consecutive summer, Cantrell's air-conditioning did not work. He felt a rage knotting in his stomach as this kid smiled at him.

Cantrell's gaze never turned from the driver in his rearview mirror. The first underpass light changed to green. The kid driving the Viper changed lanes. At the next light, the driver refused to pull parallel to Cantrell at the stoplight. The Viper driver seemed unfazed by his brazen aggression.

Cantrell stared at the driver. He spoke no words or made no gesture while observing the driver's effeminate hands with a large gold ring on the middle finger on his right hand. Cantrell imagined knocking the kid's side mirror off.

The driver made faces at Cantrell. He made the same gesture of "let's go" again to Cantrell as if to say "get over it" and "stop eyeballing me". The kid began looking over his right shoulder like he was trying to see what Cantrell stared at.

The heat inspired Cantrell to unleash some cosmic evil on this obnoxious asshole. Yet, he knew by the time he got to the Viper, there would be too many witnesses before the light changed. The light turned green.

A smog faded into the blue sky creating a colorless haze. Exhaust. Cantrell followed the Viper. The small, sporty car offended Cantrell, as if the driver believed his car was important as flesh and soul; as if the higher value of the car equated with the higher value of the person. Cantrell considered teaching the kid a lesson.

The Viper sped off with an obvious intention of losing Cantrell. The Viper raced towards the old part of town. Cantrell sped up. He knew this area. He installed electric outlets in many of these homes when the subdivision was first built. Most of the roads around here were two-lane.

They crossed over railroad tracks near houses built at least fifty years ago. Clothes of faded blues, whites and sheets hung on clotheslines amid overgrown acreage in the distance. They drove in the direction of the Tarver Equestrian Club. A festering heat enveloped Cantrell. His radio expired in January. No diversions existed from the intense summer humidity. A brain fever remains difficult to shake when only hearing one's own thoughts.

For a mile, a furniture truck between the El Camino and the Viper prevented any way for Cantrell to reposition himself behind the Viper. The El Camino still ran hard since he bought it. Fourth of July traffic jamming the roads indicated festive travelers were on the road. The Viper failed to put any real distance between them. The thick city traffic clogged old roadways.

Cantrell intended to shadow the Viper. With desperate abandon, the Viper moved through traffic, accelerating through pinches that discouraged Cantrell who decided if he should pursue this matter. On Monday, Cantrell was informed he no longer had a job. Bills would pile up. Tensions ran high. Unprovoked hostility he thought should not go unanswered. He no longer felt the heat.

Cantrell noticed no traffic or street signs he passed in order to keep up with the Viper. Cantrell wanted the driver to become tired of the chase, and lead him back to his house, or get out of the car and confront him.

He once almost lost the Viper over a hill. He thought he zoomed past a police car, but it was another government Crown Vic. Driving through an intersection leading back to the expressway the drivers exceeded the speed limit by thirty miles an hour. Cantrell drove with no awareness for his own well being. The desperate Viper driver made erratic vehicular decisions in order to shake Cantrell.

The chase continued for miles. Cantrell paid no attention to the odometer, but calibrated the chase now ran close to twenty miles long. The route became circular. The Viper drove towards the expressway. The Viper swerved across two lanes, making a sharp right on a four-lane highway.

Cantrell pursued the Viper by running two stop lights. He made it clear the Viper could not shake him. He wondered if the punk regretted his actions. The Viper turned back on to Laurel Avenue where the chase began. The Viper tried to speed away, but the holiday traffic stunted his distance. Some people have no manners, Cantrell thought.

The Viper changed lanes and made another quick right turn. Cantrell managed to turn his blinker on while making a sudden turn near a high school. He kept an eye out for pedestrians. Several miles later, they drove through an industrial district illuminated by intense heat and white light. Cantrell expected a confrontation to take place here. Cantrell noticed he wasn't wearing a seatbelt.

Cantrell understood he was wasting his time. The Viper slowed down in the left lane. Cantrell drove in the right lane. He intended to drive by the Viper with an obscene gesture. A stoplight was a hundred yards away. Cantrell was about to give up the chase until the Viper made an unexpected U-Turn at the Shiloh Baptist Church, and swerved into the opposite direction.

Cantrell refused to be eluded until he was ready to give up the chase. His actions made no sense even to himself. He intended to make the U-Turn, but Cantrell realized he would meet oncoming traffic, so he slammed on his brakes. Cantrell absorbed the collision of a maroon family van smashing into the passenger's side of the El Camino.

Shattering glass exploded throughout the inside of the car. The glass cut Cantrell's face and neck. The blood ran faster down his neck in this heat. A sharp pain burned in his left leg. A trance came over him. He did not remember closing his eyes. He made a foolish choice.

Cantrell never saw the Viper escape unscathed in the opposite direction of traffic. Everything sounded quiet for a few moments. He noticed a bearded man in the passenger seat of the family van roll down his window and ask,

"Are you all right?"

Cantrell closed his eyes again. He never heard the sirens.

The Farmer's Almanac

Founded in 1818 by David Young and Jacob Mann, the impetus for the *Farmer's Almanac* revolved around severe weather. They called 1816 "The Year Without A Summer". The original *Almanac* dates back to 1792. Ray Geiger served as the longest running editor from 1934 until he died in 1994.

The venerable *Farmer's Almanac* contains moon phases, folklore, recipes, calendars, humor, trivia, gardening tips, conservation, weather forecasts, puzzles and home remedies.

When alive, Sam's grandparents bought the *Farmer's Almanac* every year since 1939. His grandmother enjoyed ordering vegetable seeds through the mail for the garden. She also paid close attention to the natural remedies.

His grandfather read weather predictions or informative organic facts. Sam remembered once, his grandfather called out to his grandmother from his chair,

"Hey Em! Do you know today is the best day to cut your hair if you want it to grow faster?"

"Let me get my shears," Sam's grandmother responded from the kitchen.

His mother often utilized the *Almanac*. Years later, after his grandparents died, Sam bought a *Farmer's Almanac* every year. When he started his own family he found solace in a garden. He ordered seeds through the *Almanac*. The *Almanac* always served as a vital source of wisdom. Homespun science graced the pages as well as stories about rainmakers, self-taught botanists and snake oil salesmen.

He learned when to plant vegetables and cultivated a small garden. Sam enjoyed looking through the pages. He liked the way they felt. He spilled coffee on the 1996 *Almanac,* which warped and stained the pages but it gave the book character.

The *Almanac* served as the first earth grown or homegrown publication in America. The book offered advice on home essentials, natural alternatives, recipes and timeless stories. The products they advertised proved fascinating. Items such as lawnmowers, pet products, cookbooks, holistic medicine and goat milk soap were all available in the *Farmer's Almanac.*

Sam dared to imagine the hours he spent pouring over the publication. The vital book taught him to stay in touch with the Earth. It kept him grounded–close to the soil. He even admired the artwork.

Sam understood if he came across the *Farmer's Almanac* in the digital age he would have missed the book's essence. He liked being able to carry the *Almanac* anywhere. People in the 21st century seem far removed from their food, plants, water and animals.

On this overcast April evening, Sam knew he and his son would prepare to plant pepper seeds in the soft soil Thursday. Just after the rain…

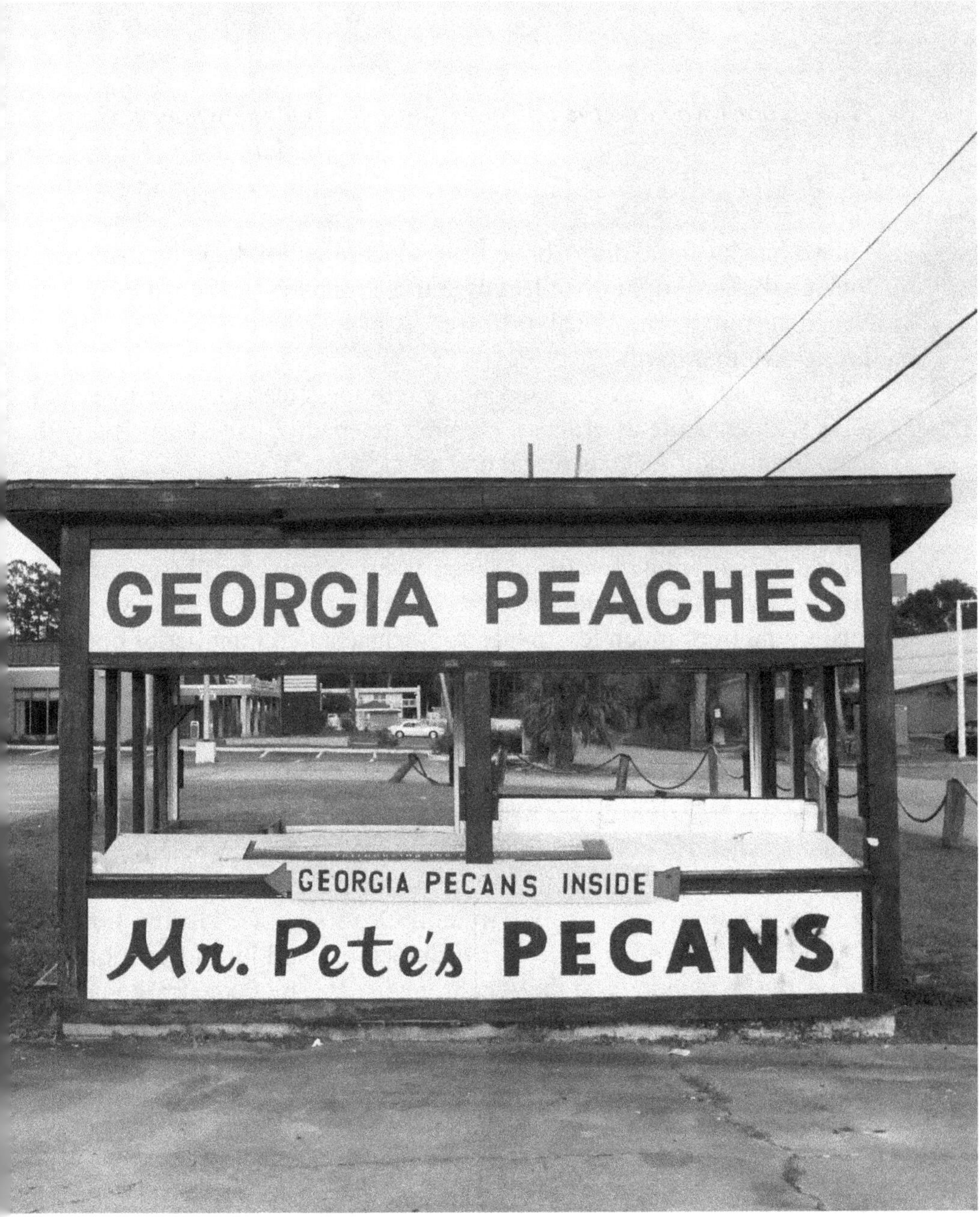
GEORGIA PEACHES
GEORGIA PECANS INSIDE
Mr. Pete's PECANS

Ballad of the Evergreen

"The clearest way into the universe is through a forest wilderness."
–John Muir

Two hawks circle high above the tree as rain clouds gather. An easy wind evokes a symphony of leaves. No man-made sounds can be heard. A mist surrounds the Eucalyptus tree. A psychedelic silence resonates through Mother Earth.

The smooth bark breathes through the limbs, green glossy leaves and veins with an acute awareness. Nature's telepathy. The tree exists with splendor as it knows a secret no one asks.

Creeping civilizations butchered trees to build everything in the modern times. Trees became victims of greed a long time ago. Strip malls appeared. Everything returns to ashes. Even instruments like guitars, pianos, cellos, drums, mandolins and others all are derived from wood of once living trees much less paper, toothpaste and a long list of obscure products–beyond the obvious.

Jeremiah sits under the tree. He smells the tree's scent. He wonders about the DNA. He read how the tree's natural oil is poisonous to most insects and animals. Protection. He runs his hand over the branch. He admired this tree. A beep goes off on his cell phone stashed in his magic leather satchel. He pulls out the phone to look at the notification.

A text from his mother. He hits his classic radio app accidentally, and the just the words of the Grateful Dead singing, "In the timbers of Fennario," played and the word 'timbers' forced him to turn off the phone, but he wondered at the synchronicity. He smelled eucalyptus. He understands these phones and gadgets have eroded his generation's perspective of reality. A disconnect between everyone's relationship with the Earth & Electricity now reaps sprawling cement mazes.

Visions of distant powerlines. Urban areas with no tree in sight. Civilization. Static. Machines. Urban noise. The boy knows the farther man is away from the earth & the trees his spirit is at hazard. So, the world's spirit is at hazard. No natural mystic exists in any concrete jungle.

"The best friend on Earth of man is the tree."
— Frank Lloyd Wright

    Under a super full moon the tree looks like a gnarled bone against the landscape. A hawk feather blows in a circle at the roots of the tree. Something approaches. Lightning flashed in the far distance like some eerie, but sure threat.

    The boy learns some hard cold facts back at home. In these modern times trouble surrounds everything and no one listens to the trees. No one is in touch with themselves–only electronic devices–visions of sonic booms, blazes, videos, strange electric currents and strange radiation breathes close to us all.

    Rochester Miles believes in nothing Evergreen. His greedy wheel rolled into motion years ago. He retains no regard for trees, nature or the earth. It's about personal gain, money, public accolades and ego. Rochester Miles plans to kill the Tree.

    Under the tree, Jeremiah's vision becomes a technicolor realization. The boy's action is the only saving grace for trees, soul and–ultimately–humanity. But, Rochester Miles won this round. Land was being cleared for a new neighborhood.

    Two weeks later, the tree was destroyed to make way for a parking lot near the new subdivision's nearby grocery store.

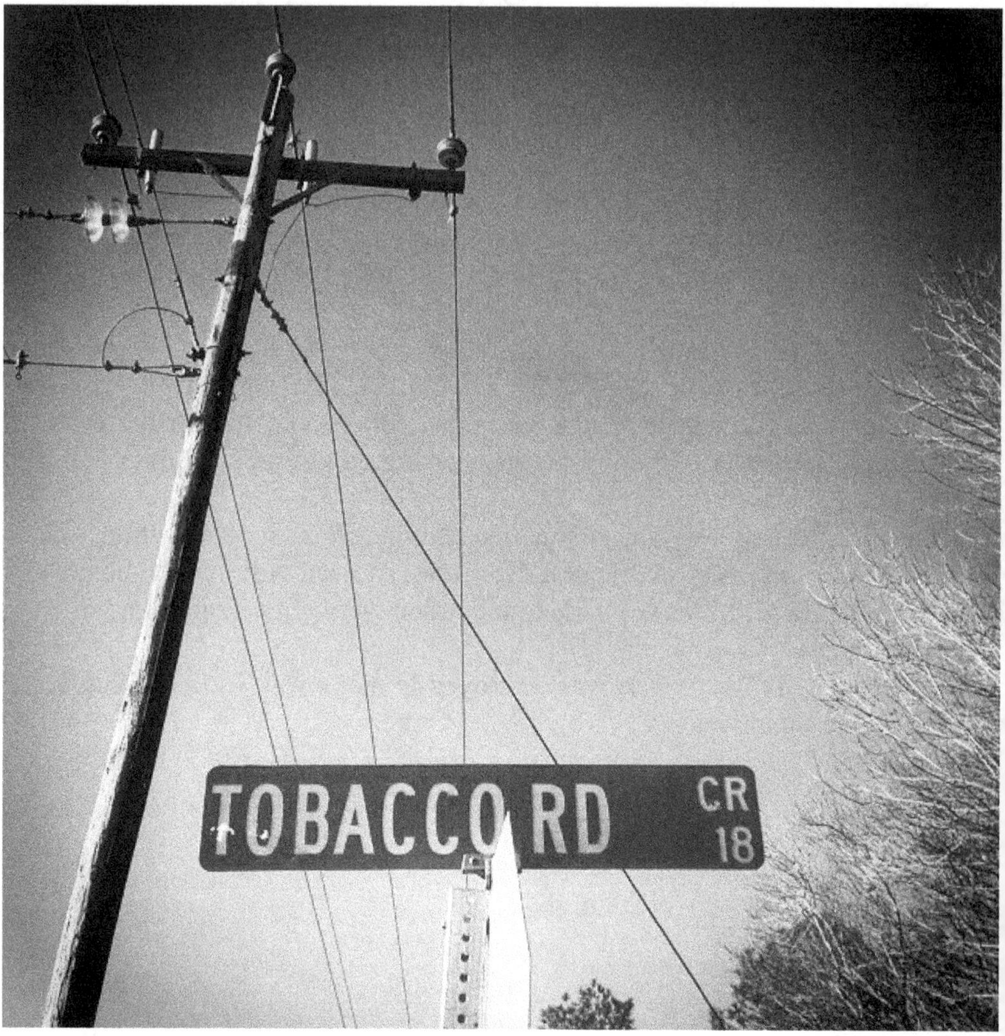
TOBACCO RD
CR
18

Tobacco Road

Wes started smoking cigarettes at thirty nine. Life's circumstances forced him to find a new vice. He dipped tobacco for years, but worried about cancer. He remembered envisioning a 'dipper' he once saw with a titanium jaw, and he knew he must quit. Cold turkey proved difficult. He started smoking to quell nicotine cravings. He traded one vice for another.

About a mile from where he worked, a tobacco shop sat in the middle of a struggling strip mall outside of Woodstock. On the way home from work, he'd stop by and buy his cigarettes. He liked an organic brand. He detested the chemical taste of Marlboros or Camels. The store called 'Tobacco Road' carried all the brands, and it provided him a chance to sample each pack to see which flavor he enjoyed the most.

Tobacco Road carried glass pipes, lighters, loose tobacco, incense, leather goods and cigars of all varieties. Wes started up a friendship with the owner named Rusty. Rusty counted as the only employee that Wes ever met at Tobacco Road.

Rusty proved accommodating. If Wes had time to kill, he'd stick around and talk to Rusty. Some days they'd talk for an hour, and on other days only a few minutes. Rusty often complained about how hard it was to stay in business.

"I'm in a bad location."

When he could afford it, Wes bought a carton of his favorite cigarettes, but he usually liked to talk to Rusty so he'd just buy a pack or two at a time. Over a couple of years, they spoke with ease to one another. Wes complained about his women troubles, and Rusty complained about business woes.

Telling troubles to strangers is not an old concept. Wes revealed most of his personal ongoings to Rusty. After a year or so, during a discussion about taxes, Rusty told Wes something he didn't tell many people.

"Hell, I was on death row for a year."

"Death row?"

"Yes, it's rare to escape death row."

Wes couldn't bring himself to inquire what sent Rusty to death row, or how he avoided execution. Wes enjoyed Rusty's perspective because he seemed to patrol the edge of reality.

"The government is not your friend. They never have been. The justice system is fucked up. Especially if you're accused of a crime you did not commit. Or if, like me, you're a veteran. It proves the system is corrupt and pathetic. It's all about money. Just to make a living is a struggle. I'm worried about the country's state of affairs–I must admit. Even more, I worry about keeping this place open."

Wes agreed, and he expressed concern.

"Well, only at your place do I shop for cigarettes. It's the only one where I can find my brand."

"You keep buying them, and I'll keep selling them."

"Deal."

Every now and then, when Wes visited Tobacco Road, Rusty talked to other customers that arrived. They looked like friends, locals or people he knew. They did not appear to be accounting-types. Wes could tell if Rusty didn't trust a patron. Wes usually waited until that person left the store and then he'd talk to Rusty.

One day, a man Wes never saw before visited Rusty. Wes stood at the end of the store scouring the incense, inspecting the pipes, the t-shirts and opened jars to smell the tobacco flavors like cherry blossom, vanilla, Tupelo honey. He even bought a french Jeep lighter he liked. He never entered the humidor because Rusty knew he didn't smoke cigars.

This customer looked ornery. He weighed around two-hundred and fifty pounds, and wore a red, white and blue cap. A long ponytail appeared from under the hat. The patron's long copper-colored beard hung to his chest. He sported a Harley Davidson tank top, cut off blue jeans, work boots, a gold watch on his right wrist and a silver bracelet on his left. The guy bought ten cartons of Marlboro reds and told Rusty,

"I'll see ya when I come back down. Take care."

"You too, bud."

Wes flicked a lighter he intended to buy, and Rusty said as he made the purchase,

"You see that guy there?"

"Yeah."

"He's an old friend of mine. He lives in Fannin County. Off the grid, as they say. He doesn't use electricity. All solar. He hates computers, and almost never turns on his burner phone. He comes into town every month for supplies. His place is damn near impossible to find. I've been there a few times. He used to be a green beret. Hard core motherfucker. He earned some money somewhere, and I swear he buried it all. No bank account. No cable. No nothing. He can't be traced. He comes here, but he's not hiding from anyone. He just lives that way. Built his house with his own hands. Let's smoke…"

For the first time they smoked inside the store together. Wes liked lighting up inside.

Almost every visit in the last few months Rusty would say as he rang up Wes' cigarettes,

"I could be closed any day now."

"Well, I hope not. I'm going to be moving out of town in two weeks. But, I'll be back once a month on business. I'll see you soon. Just hang in there."

"Take care."

Three months passed since Wes visited Tobacco Road. He relocated, but when he returned to town, he made sure to buy a carton of cigarettes from Rusty. On this late February day, Wes pulled into the familiar empty parking lot. He parked the car with a hollow feeling in his stomach. He got out of the car and walked to the front door. The place stood empty. The neon sign vanished. He peered through the windows noticing a vacant room. He already missed the jars of tobacco, Zippo lighters and incense. Closed. Gone forever. Since Wes moved out of town Tobacco Road folded.

He never saw Rusty again.

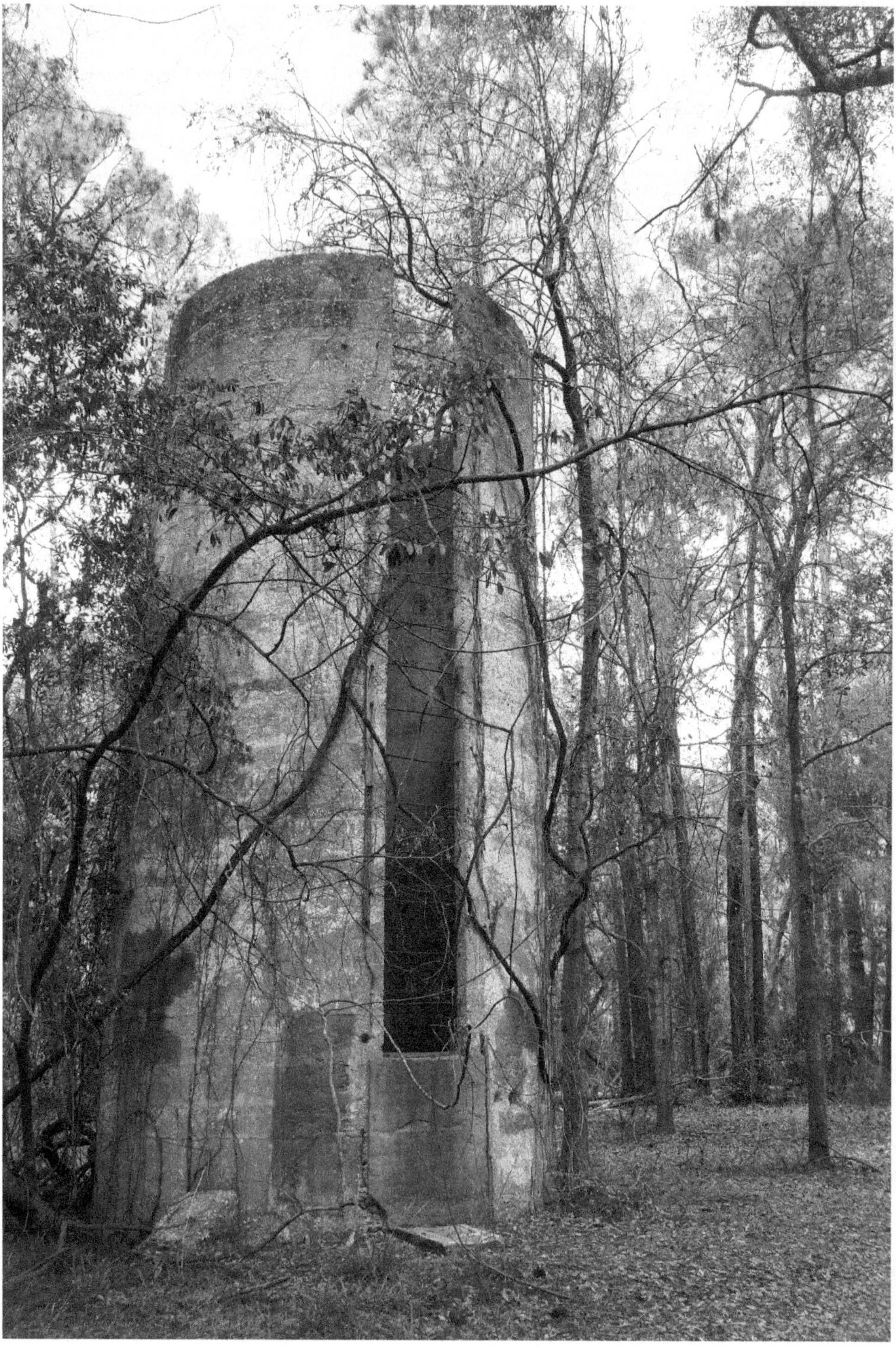

Mojo Bag

Sinister vibrations loomed in the air like an evil green fog. Eerie truths infested every passing hour. I smelled sulphur. As they say, I operated behind the eight ball. My life transformed into a series of terrible circumstances beyond my control at the hands of a criminal.

A friend, Earl, expressed concern for the dangerous situation imposed on me. He's a medicine man of sorts. Earl wanted to meet me at the Silver Sky Lounge because he felt sympathetic to my wicked circumstances and wanted to help.

He pulled up in his 1978 sky blue Ford pickup truck at sunset. Earl wore a straw cowboy hat, bolo tie, turquoise bracelet, blue jeans, shark skin cowboy boots, a forest green button-down shirt and a gold belt buckle. He looked Native American.

Once inside the dim-lit bar, Earl told me,

"Jack, in your perilous situation, an innocent man like you needs protection. I have brought serious protection."

From a beautiful hand-woven leather bag he produced the items and spread them out on the onyx bar. The gifts included: a sacred rattle bracelet from Tibet, a bag of sage, John the Conqueror root, Holy Copal from Mexico, a voodoo medicine bag from an African shaman, an alligator toenail, a feng shui crystal, an Amethyst stone, a clay incense pot from Africa and a multi-colored manta blanket from Peru.

"Now, the gator nail and medicine bag are very powerful, but it's all potent. They will protect you. Do not lose them."

"Thanks Earl."

"No problem. I gotta go. Nobody can fuck with you now."

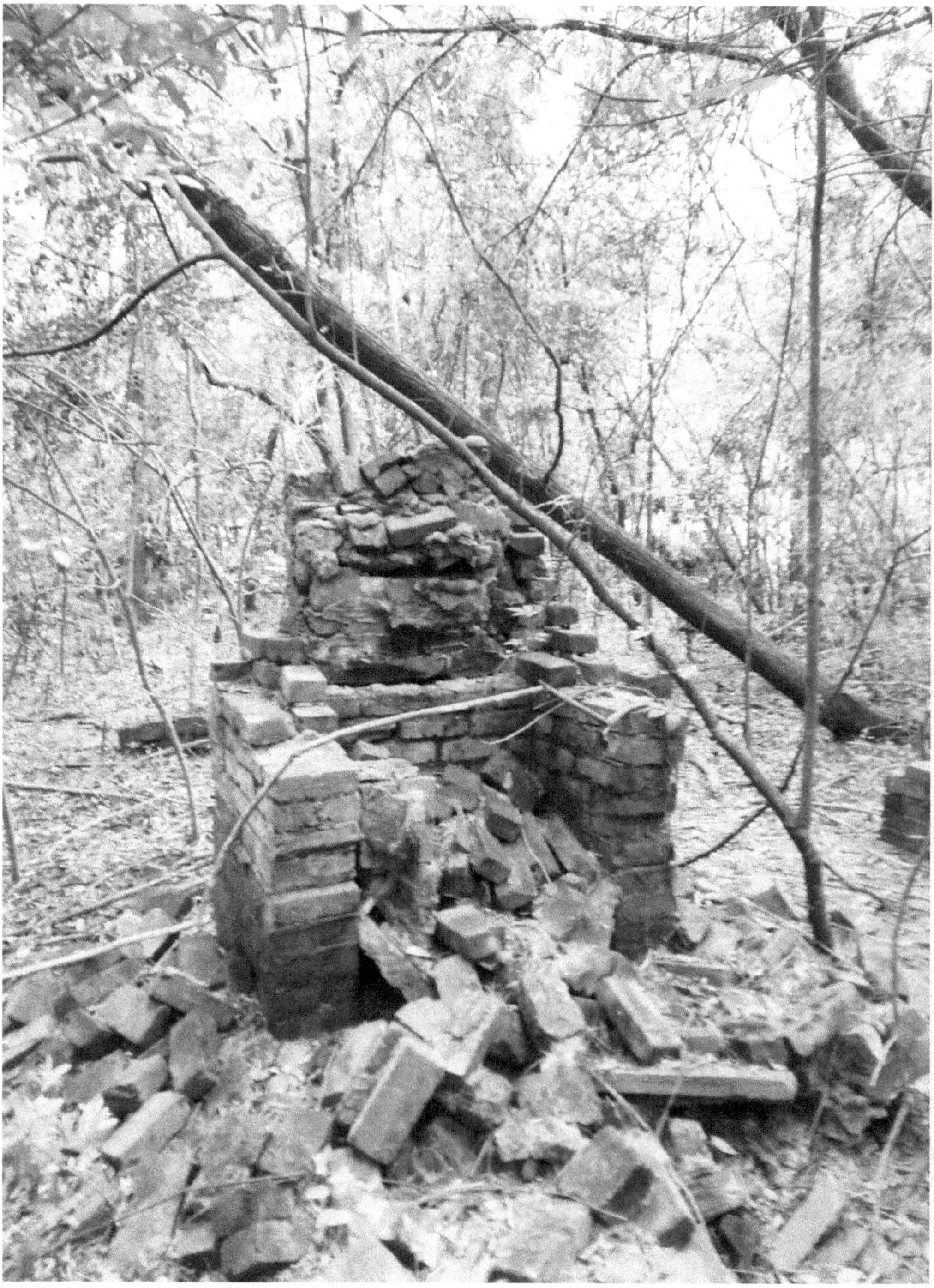

Baby Doll

Stone met a gorgeous, blue-eyed blonde at the 'Mali Restaurant', one Thursday night. She counted as a raving beauty–one of the most beautiful women he ever met. An Uber drove them back to her mediterranean-looking house in the Virginia Highlands after three hours of eating, drinking, flirting and laughing. She looked like a model. After intense sex they fell asleep in her chic, well-decorated, bedroom.

At four am, the blonde woke up gasping and held Stone tight.

"I had a terrible nightmare," she whispered. Stone awoke in an unfamiliar place, noticed the blonde's perfect face and asked,

"A nightmare?"

"The baby doll wouldn't let me talk."

"The baby doll?"

"You fucked the baby doll." Stone was now awake. He asked,

"You dreamed I fucked a baby doll?"

"The baby doll was me."

The beauty put her head back on his chest and fell back asleep. She snored a little.

Stone wondered what he got himself into with this beautiful woman.

52

Electric Blue

Above the mirror behind a liquor display, a blue neon beer sign flickered and dimmed while Luke Tarver sat at the bar. He enjoyed watching Amanda, the lovely brunette bartender, distracted by the annoying flicker of the neon light. Beautiful confusion on her face proved worth the price of any beer. Amanda's cruel curvaceous body drove most men to distraction. Her face reminded him of some killer-eyed beauty from the high quality fashion magazines.

Luke knew she'd never correlate the bothersome sign with his presence. Since he discovered no wedding ring on Amanda's finger some time ago, he considered revealing his secret to her. Luke acted like he read his newspaper while she waited on her share of admiring customers in the early evening hour.

His grandmother possessed a similar inexplicable force. No watch operated on his grandmother's wrist. It never mattered how new, expensive or inexpensive the watch, it never kept time while on her wrist and it remained a family mystery.

"Hey, how are you?"

"I'm fine. Looks like you're busy this evening."

"A little bit. What can I get you?"

"I'll have a Guinness."

Luke struggled not to stare at Amanda. He watched her glance toward the flickering neon. He smoked a cigarette while perusing the sports page. She brought the stout and gave him a smile as he handed her a twenty dollar bill. Luke felt lost on this woman. He looked back at the paper.

He remembered the first time he recognized the extent of his mysterious gift. When he was a kid he could pick four leaf clovers out of the lawn by pointing to them. This phenomenon he could articulate to no one. Later, he noticed a strange coincidence that street lamps often dimmed in his presence. Only when he was old enough to walk the streets alone could he verify this strange fact.

Luke rarely drew this phenomenon to people's attention. He didn't completely understand his power of channeling energy, insight, or foreknowledge and he always thought something might be wrong with him to invoke this mystical telepathy. At times, he could hear what people were thinking.

This strange psychic element remained a heavy burden because people he confided in often refused to believe the truth when he told it to them. His insight was a double-edged sword, but the feeling he carried with him remained opposite of an inborn fear.

Luke discovered in certain instances, radio frequencies became disrupted by his presence. The frequencies became disturbed when he felt appeared when it was least expected and often unwanted.

"Another stout?" asked Amanda after thirty minutes, pouring what remained from the bottle into his glass.

"Yes, one more," he replied, glancing up at the flickering sign to remind her it still wasn't functioning properly. A regular barfly called out to Amanda and she walked to the other end of the bar to fetch the customer a draft beer just as Luke wanted to begin a conversation with her.

Luke waited on Freddie, who was late, as usual. Freddie, an old friend of Luke's sometimes used Luke for his insight, planned an evening out on the town tonight.

Years earlier, Freddie invited several friends over to his house. In those days Freddie was an avid music enthusiast. For two months Freddie knew the Silvertones were being broadcast live on the radio and it was Freddie's intention to record the performance. A strong local frequency comforted Freddie. He planned everything--he kept three different stereo systems in his house to record the show, but the main stereo in the living room had the strongest signal.

That night, while Luke stood in the middle of the hardwood living room floor, in front of the entertainment center, they noticed reception dulled and faded while Luke stood in the room.

"That shouldn't be happening with this antennae," uttered a concerned Freddie a few minutes before showtime.

Without resistance or negativity, Luke noticed the slightest movement altered the radio's signal. He began to jest, intentionally disturbing the frequency, by moving his arm in the slightest direction, laughing.

"How in the hell are you doing that?" asked Freddie.

Even though Freddie stood amazed at this phenomenon, he wouldn't allow Luke in the living room during the performance that night.

The bar filled up. Luke could no longer read the paper. He watched Amanda. She wore shorts in mid-December weather, showing her beautiful long legs. The tight tee shirt revealed a striking anatomy. Instead of her usual ponytail, today her long, wavy dark hair hung down below her shoulders. Amanda's smile attracted many drinkers. Her eyes were blue as two pristine swimming pools. Luke began to notice Amanda watching him out of the corner of her eye.

"I've never drank stout," Amanda said to Luke when she made her way back to him. Her wide blue eyes were mesmerizing.

"It's health food, y'know."

"Health food?"

"I'm only kidding, but it's good to drink before a meal."

"I'll have to drink one and try it out," she said, smiling a telling glance as if she knew a secret, and he didn't. She made Luke wish she knew his secret. Local barflies continued vying for Amanda's attention for drink or otherwise. Luke didn't mind Freddie ran late since Amanda tended bar this evening. When she was called away by a young patron, Luke walked to the bathroom. When he returned the neon light resumed flickering.

"What's the deal with that light?" he asked Amanda, drawing her attention toward the neon sign.

"It's never done this before. It's definitely getting on my nerves."

She stared at the electric sign for a moment. He admired her long, dark eyelashes and her sly grin struck him to the bone. Luke felt the effects of the stout on his empty stomach.

"If I told you I was making that light flicker, would you have dinner with me?"

"You're crazy."

"I've been called that before. Do you think I can make it go out?"

She pursed her lips, knitted her eyebrows and gave him a look like maybe she believed him.

"No," she grinned.

"If I make the light go out, will you?"

"Okay. Yes. And if you don't?"

"Bring me a Bass Ale, and by the time you pour the beer the light will be out."

Luke stepped back from the bar where the electric currency seemed strongest. She brought the beer, and just then Freddie made his grand entrance.

"Amanda, that is a dangerous character you're consorting with. You should be very careful around this man."

Freddie sat down and Amanda said:

"He's promised to turn off the neon beer sign without touching it."

"My dear girl, I hope you didn't bet with something you couldn't pay."

When she looked up, the light was out. Luke and Amanda exchanged glances. She laughed and said,

"I get off work in an hour."

She returned to waiting on customers as if their deal never happened.

"You son of a bitch," said Freddie.

"Hey, she's my favorite bartender," Luke said.

"You know you can't go out with her tonight."

"What?"

"We've got business."

"You heard the lady. I only have one hour. All I have to do is sit back, and listen to the jukebox until then."

55

"We can make it back in time…"

"Fred, look at her."

"Come on. This is why we're here--it's close to the track."

"Don't give me that shit. If you'd show up on time for once we'd already be gone. You gave me a chance to work my courage up. Tomorrow, I'll pick a winner. I'm not focusing on horses now, and besides I just remembered you never reap luck on Thursdays."

"You're gonna squander your talent on a woman?"

Luke only looked at his friend without responding.

"Okay, scratch that, but you can always get a date with her. I'm starting to believe your only weakness is women."

"So, it's settled. We're going to the track tomorrow."

"Well, listen ol' boy. I already told Malcolm I'd put five hundred on Bound To Fade."

"You what?"

"You told me yesterday you had a feeling."

"You're pushing too hard. I never said to make that bet."

"Fuck, Luke, that's my rent money. I'll be evicted again. Don't let me down."

"Let you down? Hey, you jumped the gun. I told you…"

"Great, I'm fucked. Thanks for nothing."

Freddie stormed out of the bar.

When Amanda's shift ended, she asked him when they walked outside to his truck,

"Are you going to tell me how you turned that light off?"

"Asking the magician to reveal his tricks, eh?"

They ate dinner. An instant connection between them transcended time.

"Does your friend Freddie have a gambling problem?"

"Well, let's just say he likes taking chances."

"How did you let him down? Not that it's my business," her voice trailed off, and then she said, "But you turning that light out is my business."

Amanda smiled. Her white teeth were perfect. The lips irresistible.

Although he stayed private about it normally, Luke felt a sense of ease and relief about sharing his story, and Amanda without further questioning, smiled and said,

"I believe you, Luke Tarver. Do you not like to talk about it?"

"Not unless I want people to think I'm nuts," Luke teased.

"Fair enough."

A few hours later, Luke and Amanda rode along in his new truck and they noticed a drunken and unkempt Freddie stumbling down Elizabeth Street. Luke parked by a curb near his friend.

"Well well well. If it ain't the date that couldn't wait."

"Fred, where you been?"

"I'm trying to decide the best place to pawn my stereo equipment, but I needed a few drinks to figure it out."

"Let's go get a six pack," said Luke, allowing Freddie to climb in the back seat of his truck. They drove off and Luke noticed Amanda roll her window down a bit to diminish Freddie's unwashed scent.

"So, you guys already have a romantic glow. Amanda, has Luke told you about his freakish power yet?"

"I've seen a couple of examples."

"Yeah, the electric blue neon sign was a good one."

Luke left them talking in the truck while he ran into the liquor store. He bought a six pack of tall Budweisers, a big bag of cashews and three scratch off lottery tickets. Luke climbed back into his truck and handed the tickets to Freddie and said,

"Here, scratch these off. I believe you're a winner."

Freddie began scratching the tickets. He loved the thrill of gambling.

"Nothing on that one," he said, throwing the old ticket on the floorboard, moving to the next one licking his lips. Amanda and Luke glanced at each other and smiled as Freddie scratched the next ticket, and after a few seconds he started yelling,

"Holy fucking aces, Luke, you just won a thousand dollars. Check those numbers and make sure I'm reading it right."

"This ticket is a confirmed winner," uttered Amanda, now looking at Luke with a gaze of wild wonder. Freddie rubbed his hands together in fiendish delight.

After a few moments of silence, Luke said:

"Fred, take the money and get your rent together."

"What? Oh shit, you're kidding me! You mean it? You saved my ass again. Luke, thanks so much brother. Unless you're fucking with me…"

"Take the money, but don't ever give me that guilt trip shit again. I think we should suspend our gambling for a while after today."

"You're quitting?"

"I'm tired of all the stress it brings."

Freddie realized staring at Luke and Amanda together in the front seat that times were changing. Their gaze said it all.

"I'll never question you again. But for the Kentucky Derby next spring maybe we could have some fun. But damn. Talking about stress. Shit Luke, you're going to hate finding real work."

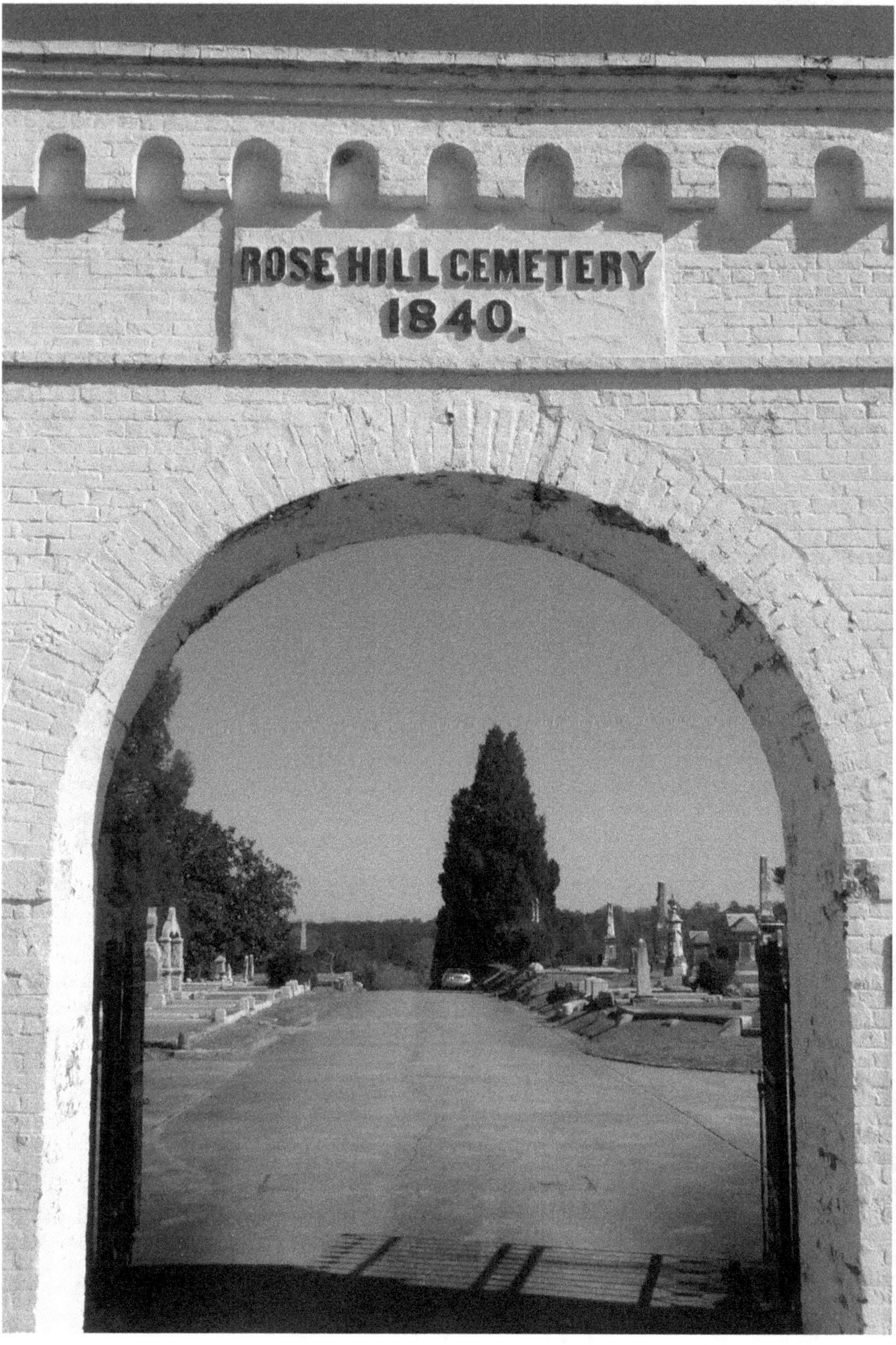
ROSE HILL CEMETERY
1840.

Rose Hill Cemetery

    Gravediggers stare at Gregg Allman's final resting place. It's a Saturday evening during early June 2017 at Rose Hill Cemetery in Macon, Georgia. Allman is buried next to his brother Duane and original bassist for the Allman Brothers Band, Berry Oakley. Rose Hill Cemetery was founded in 1840. A railroad separates the cemetery from the Ocmulgee River. The Allmans' graves face the river. It's been quite some time since this many people flocked to Macon.
    The cemetery contains a jewish section, a slave section and a confederate soldier section. The Allman Brothers Band used to play acoustic guitars at night in Rose Hill. In recent years, family members paid for a fence to prevent vandals from desecrating the musician's headstones.
    Now the Allman gravesite expanded. Gregg's resting place sits near his brother Duane and the Allman's bassist Berry Oakley on a little grassy hill .
    Gregg Allman's funeral transpired earlier today.

Gravediggers:

Larry Bowman–56, foreman, Maconite. White. Stocky. Gray beard.

Sam Jackson–31, new employee. Black. Tall. Skinny. Wears wire-rimmed glasses.

Rex Miller–27, white guitar player. Short. Skinny. Scraggly beard. Braves hat. Maconite.

Tony Diaz–40, Mexican-American. Clean shaven. In shape. Moved to Macon when he was 12.

Larry: Well, I'm proud of us all. This one is historic and personal.

Rex: Damn, I can't believe all three of them are right here. Hell Larry, you turned me onto the Allman Brothers.

Sam: My father used to play those records with Aretha Franklin, Wilson Pickett, King Curtis and Herbie Mann. That's how I knew about Duane Allman. I never heard much of the Allman Brothers before then.

Tony: My uncle used to drive my aunt crazy with the "Mountain Jam" when we moved here, and that's when I got turned onto *Eat A Peach*.

Larry: They touched us and everybody from all walks of life. Since the sun is setting, let's all have a cigarette. This day won't come again. Hell, even Jimmy Carter showed up. They go way back.

They sat behind the graves staring out towards the Ocmulgee River. Highway 75, right across from the railroad tracks, can be heard in the distance.

Tony: This is a historic spot. Think of all the people that have and will come to these graves. It's spiritual.

Rex: Brothers. Side by side.

Sam: You can feel something here.

Larry: I never thought I'd bury Gregg Allman. I've been visiting Rose Hill Cemetery since I was 12. My dad went to the Byron Pop Festival up the road in 1970. I played all those records over and over. Hell, they wrote "In Memory of Elizabeth Reed" and "Little Martha" based on graves in this cemetery.

Rex: It's kind of mind-blowing.

Sam: Maybe they can hear us.

Larry: If they can–I'd want them to know they got me through a lot of times–good and bad.

Rex: Hell, people my age don't know good music.

Sam: You got that right.

Larry: They were one of the first integrated rock & roll groups. They made you proud to be southern again.

Tony: Being here makes me want to hear their music.

Larry: As the story goes they'd come here and play acoustic guitars at night.

Sam: Hanging out with the hoot owls.

Larry: God bless them all.

Tony: There goes the train...

Flirting With Arson

Elijah decided to wash his truck one warm Tuesday afternoon in February. His neighbor to the right of his property was dealing with a plumber today. Elijah's street, Sycamore Avenue, counted as one of the older homes in this neighborhood. Both of the two-story homes across the street were recently sold by the original owners for a half of million dollars. The neighborhood, built in the 1950s, now ranked as prime real estate.

The new homeowners on the opposite side of the street spent thousands of dollars to implement significant changes to the house and landscapes. A tree cutting service completed drastic alterations regarding old oak and pine trees hovering over the house.

The other house directly across the street from Elijah, owned by a wealthy homebuilder, allowed his thirty-five year old son to rent the house. Last weekend, the son welcomed two new male roommates.

From what Elijah gathered–the fellows across the street were a wild bunch. Occasionally, he'd see a female visitor from time to time. They employed a maid.

Two months ago, Elijah pulled into his driveway and noticed someone ran over the neighbor's mailbox across the street. The neighbors appeared unconcerned. A week later they replaced the post, but mounted the same smashed mailbox back on the new post. Strange.

Elijah stepped outside to wash his truck. He smelled the early-blooming Camellia bush near the water hose. Before he turned on the water faucet near the garage, Elijah noticed smoke rising from his peripheral vision. A fire started on the left side of his neighbor's house across the street.

At first, Elijah thought they might be burning leaves, but then he noticed one of the new wooden columns on the front porch burning. Elijah didn't turn on the water. He pulled out his cellphone. Black smoke moved skyward.

Elijah ran across the street and noticed a red gas can ablaze on the front porch. As soon as Elijah pounded on the neighbor's front door, he heard a popping sound as the flames grew higher. Elijah thought the gascan may explode. Just as he was about to call 911, the neighbor answered the door.

The new neighbor, a short fellow of maybe thirty years old with short dark hair, wore blue jeans and a t-shirt. He seemed unfazed by Elijah's frantic knocking.

"Hey man, you got a fire here!"

"Oh, my cigarette must have caught something on fire."

The neighbor casually walked into the house and fetched a dog bowl full of water. He threw it on the fire, and the flames licked higher. He appeared unfazed by his roommate's burning house. The neighbor walked a little faster back inside. The fire spread to the wood beam supporting the roof. Elijah took it upon himself to grab a metal pole that leaned up against the house and scraped the debris compost–composed of beer bottles and whatever else away from the house. Elijah felt like he was in a Peter Sellers movie. He envisioned being blown up helping his dumb neighbor.

The bottom of the last column wood resembled charcoal. The bricks even turned black, and wood damage on the side of the house became obvious. After a few rushed trips for water, the fire disappeared.

"Man, thanks," the neighbor said.

"What's your name?"

"Mike."

"Mike, I'm Elijah. I live across the street. Nice to meet you. I almost called the fire department. I didn't know if you were sleeping."

"Yeah, my bedroom is right there."

The neighbor pointed to the blackened wall.

"Is this your house?"

"It's my roommate's–he's also my boss. He's asleep."

Mike appeared unfazed about the fire. Elijah wondered what Mike's boss, friend and landlord might think about this damage to the house, which came close to destruction.

"Well, nice to meet you."

"Thanks again."

"You're welcome."

Elijah saved his neighbor's house from burning down. He wondered if New Neighbor Mike felt satisfied with these events. Maybe he flirted with arson? Anyway, Elijah fulfilled his good deed for the day. He'd keep an eye on these weirdos.

JOhnny CASH'S
1946 1½ Ton Ford
was used in the
Murder in Coweta
Couty MOVIE 1983
Johnny Cash
&
Andy Griffin

The Crew

"Hey man, you wanna run wid de big dogs you gotta get off the porch," said Big Al with an evil grin.

Big Al's sleeveless white tee shirt displayed his tattooed arms. Big Al weighed around two-hundred and sixty pounds. His chocolate-colored skin revealed a road map of scars. A smooth, three-inch scar rested above his right eyebrow. A large burn scar smeared across his skin on his thick right forearm. Big Al Spat. He smoked a Newport cigarette, and watched a new co-worker struggle to move a heavy piece of office furniture from a moving truck.

"Dat 'lil muthafucker gonna get his due," Sweet Lou echoed Big Al's sentiment concerning the new guy on the job.

Sweet Lou's physique was that of a boxer, almost viperous. He wore a Mephisto beard. His dark hands appeared scarred and strong. Sweet Lou wore his dark, walnut-colored fingernails long and sharp. His eyes looked like black marbles, hidden within deep sockets of his bullet shaped skull that displayed a malevolent shine.

Sweet Lou and Big Al thrived on confrontation. Intimidation. Earning enemies unfazed them. They lived together at the county rehabilitation farm.

It ranked as the hottest day in May in seventy-seven years. The black Georgia asphalt simmered a wicked heat, causing tempers to flare. The crew of fifteen workers waited for the last few items on the truck to be moved into a commercial office space. Some of the crew worked for a moving company, some worked for a temporary agency and several were rehabilitating felons. The felons were allowed to work and save money while living in a halfway house.

Tractor-trailer trucks stood parked in long corridors of corporate buildings and warehouses for the moving crews to unload office furniture and equipment. The crew traveled in separate company vans. Seven of them rode in one van: Tyler, the supervisor: Jerry, a part-time country singer: a big, violent eighteen year old they called The Kid: a temp worker they called Doc: Sweet Lou, Big Al and a new guy.

The new guy was a small, white fellow with a crew cut. A cleft palate dominated his face. A nasty scar marked his nose and lips, rendering his speech difficult to understand. The sun shined at a zenith casting hot white heat. Only dead, humid air pressed down on the simmering ground. Before lunch, the crew unloaded four tractor trailers full of furniture.

The country singer asked the supervisor to drive him through the bank to deposit money. The drive-thru bank lines were long at lunch hour. The singer decided to jump out of the truck and wait inside. The six other members sweated in the hot unventilated truck.

"Take care of personal shit on your time motherfucker," hissed Big Al, lighting a Newport.

"Hillbilly motherfucker", said Sweet Lou.

"This is bullshit. This is my fucking time."

The crew became intolerant in the parking lot. A festering heat enveloped the van. Big Al commented on each woman leaving the bank.

"Look at this shit," said Sweet Lou pointing at the new guy eating his lunch from a brown bag.

The new guy tried to be invisible. The cleft palate, a curse from childhood, would haunt him to his grave. He long since tired of insulting jeers and curious stares. It angered him especially when strangers made fun of him. Every day someone reminded him of his face.

Sweet Lou watched the new guy eating, like a snake examining a mouse. Big Al began staring at the new guy whose neck began to turn red.

"You got any teeth?" Big Al asked with a wicked sneer, blowing smoke through his flared nostrils. The new guy chewed his sandwich with an embarrassed look. The rest of the crew turned away. The new guy's face had small, damp chewed bits of sandwich around his mouth, making Big Al grimace with disgust. The new guy muttered he did have teeth.

"Where are they?" asked Big Al, as he and Sweet Lou broke into a chorus of laughter. The new guy, unable to eat under scrutiny, began coughing and sputtering. Big Al opened the van door and jumped out laughing. He moved quickly.

"If you puke on me motherfucker, I'll fuck you up."

"Idth, athmah–nif you'd us eave ne na fuck anone," wheezed the new guy, trying to regain a normal breathing pattern.

"Then wipe that nasty shit off your mouth before I puke all over you."

"Can't even understand the motherfucker," said Sweet Lou. A feeling of genuine pity pervaded the rest of the crew, but no one spoke or looked at the other.

The country singer jumped back in the van. He apologized for making them wait.

"That's the last time I'm taking you anywhere on my lunch break hillbilly ass," said Sweet Lou.

"Let's go eat some Q," said Big Al, and it was agreed.

For the rest of the afternoon, the new guy remained silent. No one spoke to him. He never showed up again for work.

When the phone rang at five AM, Doc knew it was work calling. They told him to be at the warehouse in one hour. He dressed and arrived at the site with five minutes to spare. Severe dread hounded his senses in the early gray dawn. A lonely, ruthless day lie ahead. His schedule today counted as twelve hours, but he knew in two weeks he'd receive a much better assignment tailored for his specific skill set.

Each crew member's mood appeared more irascible and unpredictable in the morning. Doc noticed the guy with the cleft palate didn't make it today. He didn't make it a week. Some made it only one day. He wondered how long he'd endure this assignment.

The day seemed to pass with an anonymous swiftness. Towards the end of the day, the crew charted only one more truck to unload, but it was not at the same location. The crew drove the company vans to another workstation. Crew members climbed into the familiar vans with usual demeanors.

Doc noticed no one sitting in the van front seat. He almost changed his mind before he sat down, but he figured this one time wouldn't matter. Then he heard the Kid call from the warehouse,

"I know ain't nobody sitting in my seat."

The kid weight about two hundred pounds, dumb, mean and strong as an ox. He flaunted his strength to everyone except Big Al and Sweet Lou. The kid walked up to Doc who was reading a newspaper and said,

"Get up."

The crew's attention shifted towards Doc, who knew if he caved in then he'd lose respect on the crew. Doc decided if the Kid touched him, he'd headbutt the Kid.

"I'm not moving."

"Get up."

"When I get out of this seat, you can sit here all you want. But I'm not moving."

"Fuck you temp guys. I been here longer than you."

"You sound like a bitch in heat."

"Get up."

"I'm not moving."

The kid climbed into the backseat, and said:

"You can sit there now. Next time, I'm going to do something about it."

"You better do something about it now."

Doc stared at the Kid with hate. He prepared to fight. The crew did not speak. Doc felt furious that he had to earn a living by working with these dangerous idiots.

The supervisor climbed into the van, and said time to go. All the van doors closed.

"Both you white boys shut the fuck up," grinned Big Al, flexing his pectoral muscles as a sign of authority. Doc felt the menacing vibrations around him. They rode to the next designated location. Big Al squinted at Doc through cigarette smoke, and said aloud as he pointed:

"See, motherfuckers like ol' Doc here are dangerous. He could be anything he wants–doctor, lawyer or motherfucking president. But ol' Doc here likes to run wid de bad bloods. That's what makes him dangerous. All that gray hair on your young ass–you a wise motherfucker Doc, but you don't weigh much, dig?

Sweet Lou flicked his cigarette ash out the window. As they drove to the next loading site, a sense of violence lingered in the air. Doc sat forward in the passenger seat. He wondered how long he could hang on to this job, support a family and not become damaged in a permanent capacity by his violent co-workers. Doc refused any more dangerous tests. The next day he called the agency, and requested a new job.

Blind Willie McTell

*"And I know no one can sing the blues like
Blind Willie McTell." – Bob Dylan*

I started driving up Georgia Highway 17. Somewhere between Brunswick and Darien, Georgia, where marsh sits on both sides of the two-lane highway, I turned up the volume to the Blind Willie McTell *Atlanta Twelve String* CD I was playing to hear him singing "You just as well to live a Christian/You got to die…"

For this trip, my intent was to visit Blind Willie McTell's hometown in Thomson, Georgia. Most people know a Blind Willie song the Allman Brothers Band or Taj Mahal covered called "Statesboro Blues". Perhaps the most gifted of all bluesmen, McTell always ranked as a favorite artist of mine.

I planned to take Highway 95 to Highway 16 until the Swainsboro exit. Then I'd drive through rural Georgia towns such as Blundale, Wadley, Aldreds, Louisville, Wrens and eventually McTell's hometown of Thomson, Georgia.

Blind Willie played a 12-string guitar like few other players and his lyricism remains brilliant in a sad, humorous or any spiritual context even today. I felt compelled to visit the rural environs McTell knew so well only sixty years ago. Thomson existed as one of McTell's sanctuaries, so to speak. The last time I visited Thomson was to attend the Blind Willie McTell Blues Festival a decade ago.

Willie Samuel McTier was born in either 1901 or 1898 (sources vary) in a small home just south of downtown Thomson. Born blind, McTell endured an unstable home life. His father's intense gambling and drinking forced his mother to take young Willie with her to Stapleton, Georgia. Around 1907, they settled in Statesboro, Georgia, where a thriving lumber and turpentine business offered employment opportunities.

McTell had plenty of aunts, uncles, and cousins on both sides of his family who helped take care of him. Eventually, they helped McTell during his music travels. He started playing guitar at 10. McTell attended the state school for the blind in Macon, Georgia, but he also attended schools in North Carolina, Michigan and New York. McTell's education far exceeded the average African-American child of the time.

The calluses he developed from playing guitar made it difficult for him to read braille. His family proved somewhat musical and McTell eventually owned his signature 12-string guitar. He learned different styles, songs and scales he'd later use in his vast repertory.

McTell moved to Atlanta in the early 1930s. He married a woman named Kate in 1934 and earned enough money to put her through nursing school. McTell proved self-reliant and memorized every street in each city he visited or lived. He never allowed his handicap to hold him back concerning his music, money or travels. McTell's soulful endurance must be noted.

Sometimes Kate traveled with McTell on his musical tours that consisted of Atlanta, Augusta, Savannah and Macon. He knew people in each town that could assist him with gigs, lodging and food during a dangerous time for a blind traveling black musician in the Deep South. On occasion, McTell performed with a pianist or another guitarist like his buddy Curly Weaver at barrelhouses, parties and juke joints. For the most part, McTell operated as a solo artist.

Some of McTell's nicknames (although he never recorded under them) were Blind Sammie, Hot Shot Willie, Barrelhouse Sammie, Willie McTier, Blind Doogie and Pig N Whistle Red among, I'm sure, others. McTell cultivated a broad catalogue of songs, ballads and blues that he played for black and white, rich and poor audiences at barbecues, medicine & minstrel shows, proms, parties, vaudeville theatres, railroad stations, fraternity parties and even churches.

McTell teamed up with Blind Willie Johnson in Atlanta where they recorded together. In the 1940s, McTell traveled through Georgia with a group of blind musicians from Atlanta. In his life, McTell recorded 120 of his own songs in 14 separate recording sessions. One of McTell's steadiest jobs existed at an Atlanta drive-in barbecue joint called The Pig 'N' Whistle.

In the 1950s, he also played steady-paying gigs at a place called The Blue Lantern. He made pretty good money. Blind Willie operated as a professional of the highest order. His travels took him to all the major cities in the South such as Memphis, New Orleans and Atlanta, but he also ventured to New York City and San Francisco.

He often followed the tobacco market from Georgia up to North Carolina where he could play at warehouses, auctions and hotels. He also performed for snowbirds in my neck of the woods--the Georgia Sea Islands--and even down in Miami.

I took the Swainsboro exit, which turns into highway 57 for a little while. I started listening to McTell's early recordings as I admired the landscape, abandoned barns, old vacant gas stations, deserted homes and virgin landscape, all which emitted a rural glory. I wondered what these places looked like to McTell in his day because I was sure he traveled this same highway. A light yellow dust of pollen covered everything.

I stopped for gas in Wrens, Georgia. I went inside and bought a coffee-flavored energy drink, a bag of cashews and a bottle of water. I knew Thomson was only about 20 miles up the road. This was, indeed, Blind Willie country. The March weather proved beautiful. It was 70 degrees. The past couple of years weak winters caused azaleas and camellias to bloom early in Georgia.

I ate the cashews in the parking lot after I pumped the gas. I took a swig of water and opened the coffee drink. I drove off slowly staring at a field of pine trees. I was in no hurry. I knew in the mid-1940s McTell left his wife Kate and began living with a woman named Helen in Atlanta where he could rely on the Pig 'N' Whistle and The Blue Lantern for steady gigs without constant traveling. Damn, he could play. I sang along to his early recording of "Love Changing Blues": "If my love don't change/There gonna be some stealin' done."

During this time, McTell made two landmark recordings in Atlanta. My favorite two were always the *Atlanta Twelve String* and *Blind Willie's Last Session*.

At the time, McTell preached at an Atlanta church. His faith laced his later compositions. Helen died in 1958 and McTell's health declined. He was diabetic and he drank too much and suffered a mild stroke the following year. His family brought him back to Thomson.

McTell suffered a more severe stroke in August of 1959, and he died in a Milledgeville, Georgia, hospital. Some say he got a bit excited at a party he was playing and collapsed. Blind Willie McTell left this world at 61.

Before I knew it, I pulled into downtown Thomson. It's a small place, but it has modern day establishments like Bojangles, Walmart and Waffle House. It's like any small American town. I kept finding myself trying to see this little town as Blind Willie would have seen it eighty or even sixty years ago. Where did the juke joints used to be? Probably eight thousand people live in this town. Thomson is called the "Camellia City of the South". Thomson, of course, served as a depot for the Georgia Railroad. James Brown's hometown, Augusta, served as the city nearest Thomson.

I found a Hampton Inn, and decided to stay the night. After I checked in I wanted to walk around downtown. I also planned to visit McTell's grave at the nearby Jones Grove Baptist Church Cemetery about 10 miles south of town. I never visited his grave before.

I ate at Ivery's Restaurant on Railroad Street, which is a memorable 'all you can eat' soul food buffet. I admired the Martin Theatre that was built in the early 1950s that McTell would've passed many times. The town showcases a "McTell's 12-String Strut" now, which is a public art project.

The Thomson Depot serves as a venue for the community. They hold a lot of weddings there. I wondered if those bricks on the Depot were the same ones McTell saw. His spirit seemed close. He once stood on these grounds, which emanates a positive light and vibration. And Thomson hosts the Blind Willie Blues Festival every year, God bless 'em.
I felt good, but it was a short lonely drive through the empty landscape to McTell's final resting place. The Jones Grove Baptist Church is a little white building that sits off Happy Valley Road. His large headstone features a guitar and engraved upon the stone:

Blues Legend
Blind Willie McTell
Born Willie Samuel McTier
May 5, 1901
Died
August 19, 1959

I touched the cold tombstone. A breeze blew across the landscape. Birds chirped all around. It was very quiet. Peaceful. I bet Willie liked this spot. Daylight Savings Time transpired yesterday, so I knew I had an extra hour of light. I tried to channel McTell's perseverance and pure inspiration into my own life–to overcome obstacles. I decided to sing one of his songs over his grave: a favorite of mine–"Dyin' Crapshooters Blues". I heard myself sort of rapping his lyrics:

"Send poker players to the graveyard
Dig my grave with the ace of spades
I want twelve police in my funeral march
Playing blackjack leading the parade
I want the judge who jailed me fourteen times
Pair of dice in my shoes
Let a deck of cards be my tombstone
I got the dying crapshooters blues."

"Rest easy, Willie," I said as I took one last glimpse at his grave, and headed back to the car. Somehow I knew Blind Willie McTell would accompany me back to Thomson just before sunset like some friendly ghost.

Black Flag Manifesto

Max Jacobs read the email. The writer informed Jacobs in the elevator yesterday he'd give Jacobs a vague outline of the story he pitched a few weeks ago regarding corruption at the highest level of a powerful energy company. The writer informed Jacobs the story contained ominous implications, and might cause some people to lose their jobs, get run out of the country or go to jail. This writer operated as a freelancer, and his sharp insight often lost him jobs, but his instinct always proved right. He wrote brutal truths. Jacobs put on his reading glasses and read the email sent two hours ago.

"Jacobs, this is the gist: This stands as Corruption at the highest level. No mercy for these rats now in this maze of fear--this malignant psychosis on a corporate level deserves a blizzard of shame. They impose ugly ways to live for innocent people. We're talking about poison water.
I know the risks. I know I'm operating without a net. But this evil shit must be exposed. It's beyond criminal. We are NOT in the forgiveness business.

"I need your permission to tell the story about this circle of traitors and this deadly secret regarding the environment they're hiding. How does the other half live in their evil world? Let's find out and unleash the dogs of war on these liars, thieves and motherfuckers smiling with a sinister glint in their dead eyes. They love to betray and lie--to win at any cost. There is no loyalty among them. Say nothing. I'm in possession of a quite damning harddrive that explains everything and connects every dot. Just Venmo the expense money. A darker end for a dirty need lurks in this critical story. Let me raise the black flag and begin slitting throats, okay? Send word. Jack.

Jacobs closed his laptop. He grabbed his cell phone and called his editorial manager and told her to prepare space for the writer's story "two weeks from today". Jacobs then called the writer, and informed him to write the story and it will be published.

Ten days later, before the story was submitted, the writer became a 'missing person'.

Ides of March

The satanic overture fell on the Ides of March 2013. That day, Lily--the Snake–texted,

"Please pick me up. I need you. Bad."

Five months passed since they spoke. Cotton felt bored. He felt tempted by Lily the Snake, and he betrayed his instinct by agreeing to meet her. Cotton got off work and picked up the Snake. They visited two bars for one drink (although she'd been drinking all day) without any real drama, but her dark side simmered just beneath the surface.

The Snake spent most of the evening complaining about her kids and her ex-husband. Cotton knew her story well because since 2008 this serpent existed as a menace to one degree or another in his life. She personified a straight-up nightmare of a woman. Cotton always championed women as equals, but Lily the Snake proved to be a different set of molecules.

The Snake pleaded to spend the night with Cotton. She drank from a bottle of wine she brought along for the ride. The Snake acted dramatic once they left the bars and arrived at his house. At one point, the Snake claimed she intended sleeping in the car. He already regretted bringing her to his house.

"Please don't be melodramatic tonight. Come inside. Watch some TV, and relax," Cotton reasoned.

Once in the house, the Snake started kissing and undressing Cotton with an unusual aggression. Twenty minutes after sex, the Snake became outraged over Cotton's friend–Larry Starke–who in a case of mistaken identity believed the Snake was her (much hated) sister one night in a bar.

"What is that guy's name?"

"How many times do I have to tell you? Rory Davis. Why are you going on about this again?"

"Larry is lying to you!"

"What are you talking about? You were the one in the bar with the guy. And you're asking me his name?"

At this point, Cotton watched the evil black dilation in the Snake's eyes. Rage boiled in her face. She stood up, got in his face and said with clenched fists,

"Sometimes I just want to punch you in the face. Take me home."

"Call a taxi. I'm over the legal limit. And if you punch me in the face, I don't care how you get home."

She hit Cotton twice–hard as she could with her fist in his left jaw. Flashpoint. The Snake called 911. Then she also managed to call her parents. Suddenly everything took on a surreal quality beyond comprehension.

"Get the fuck out you crazy bitch!"

She broke a mantle hanging on the wall. She ran to the back of the house and sat in a corner. Cotton couldn't get Lily the Snake out of the house. The cops called back. Then her mother called.

Cotton demanded she leave. Either she could leave with her parents or the cops. His heart and mind raced. The Snake demonstrated violent and abusive behavior before (she once stabbed him in the chest with a pen), but this proved the final straw. Her mother called, and Cotton expressed years worth of frustration with the Snake's drinking and her family's attitude towards Cotton in general as a scapegoat. When the cops arrived Cotton met them at the front door.

The big, crew-cut cop asked Cotton questions like how long did he know the Snake? Did they have children? Did they live together?

"Is she still in the house?"

"I don't know."

"Check all the closets and every room."

Cotton looked for the Snake in every room. She was not in the house or on property. She caused a scene and departed–presumably out walking in the streets with no shoes in the cold air at 2:30 AM. She left her shirt and only wore a jacket. Crazy bitch. Pure, unadulterated disrespect, alcoholism and lunacy transpired again with this individual and Cotton invited it. Here he was with the cops on his doorstep explaining her crazy shit, and she was nowhere to be found. Typical.

It felt like a setup. He explained the story to the cop. He only drank two beers since he got off work at 9:45 PM, and one since they got to his house. It was 2:30 AM now. By the time the cops and the Snake's parents left the clock read 3 AM. The Snake disappeared. The cop gave Cotton a case number on his card and informed him he could press charges Monday if he desired.

Cotton locked every door and turned off all the lights. About fifteen to twenty minutes later he heard a commotion outside the house. He heard her parent's familiar truck, and yelling. It sounded like the Snake saying 'Fuck You'.

Cotton felt nervous. Wrecked-out. Bad nerves on a sleepless night. Was the Snake yelling at her parents? Did they find her walking back to his house and forced her to go with them? He thought of all the shit over the years he'd endured over the Snake and the lunacy she created. What a fucking waste of time.

The next morning, Saturday, Cotton told Larry the story,

"Go to the fucking police and file charges! That woman is fucking sick in the head. Goddamn I keep telling you this. How many more years will you put up with this crazy bitch?"

Cotton wanted to vomit. It proved hard to fathom the sinister facts that transpired less than twelve hours before. The Snake's evil insults from years on end echoed through his mind. Years of her toxic narcissism, craving men's attention, temper tantrums, jealousies, lies, drug addiction, alcoholism, mental illness and general meanness ended.

She even once abandoned Cotton and his eight-year old daughter to score coke, and yet he returned to her two weeks later during a weak moment. He'd been warned. Now, he decided never again would he speak to such a reptile.

Cotton finally decided to hate the Snake. They'd not been a couple in years. The Snake's dangerous insanity must be avoided. Cotton knew he made a mistake answering the Snake's call last night.

Let the buzzards come home to roost on old sister midnight. From Hell's heart I'll stab at thee, eh? Cotton lived far beyond sick of her lethal jests and drunken shamelessness. He now felt like a metaphorical assassin on this brain-damaged slut.

The joke's over. He vowed this savage night would strengthen his work, values, views on virtues, vice, friendship, ties to loved ones, resolve and true love. Revenge is a dish best served cold. There is no remedy for terminal craziness. Good riddance. Cotton shed her dark and slippery ways. A struggle between light and dark became clear. And to think he once cared about her made him sick, ashamed and angry.

But, Cotton didn't press charges against her on Monday. He decided to never speak to her again. He wanted no legal ties to the Snake. He just wanted her to leave him alone.

Ten days later, by chance, still not having heard from her–Cotton saw the Snake drinking in a bar with another man. Cotton, like a fool, expected an apology in the following days after the Ides of March, but it never came. The Snake was a sociopath by clinical definition.

The Snake was already trolling for a new victim. Looking for a new man to facilitate her toxic ways or to seek Cotton's attention. He didn't see her at first, but after saying hello to a couple of folks Cotton realized he could've reached out and touched her. They looked into the other's eyes. The Snake looked haggard, spiteful and crazy. Cotton's stare said fuck you. You're welcome, I didn't throw your slut ass in jail. Cotton felt an extreme prejudice against the Snake. He walked out of the bar.

Any thoughts of the Snake made him nauseated. He understood it may take years to reconcile or absolve the abuse he incurred. Cotton earned the right–and his friends more than agree–to hate that sick bitch. No more sentimental nonsense. He knew the face of Evil, and felt pissed off at himself for even answering her call.

Cotton saw the Snake a week later when he stepped out to eat with an old friend Donny on Easter Sunday. They dined at a Mexican restaurant and the Snake sat at the bar alone all dolled up. The Snake did not stay long once she noticed them. Still no apology, remorse or even acknowledgement of her extreme craziness from three weeks ago. It was Easter Sunday, and her evil deed was complete.

Donny noticed Cotton's hands shaking as he drank his glass of beer. He felt sick. They left.

Cotton operated beyond the call of duty on and off for three years regarding many changes he endured with this serpent. For three years he was willingly used, manipulated and abused–voluntarily at times–by a mentally ill, drunk, drug-addict, bipolar, compulsive liar, double-dealer, bar tramp, slut and borderline psychotic. Hard facts. In the beginning he thought he could help her. Clearly, all they'd been through meant nothing. At a certain point he quit caring about her.

In 2011, he left the Snake for another woman.

"Now you belong to the dead," said the Heroine from *The Mummy*. And Cotton felt the same way. His original feeling for the Snake transformed into the opposite. He knew why he left her for another woman two years ago because besides her addiction and mental illness she always tried to make an ass out of him at every turn.

The Ides of March scene played over and over in Cotton's mind those following weeks. One month later, on April 15, he finished his shift and drove the usual route home. He pulled out of the parking lot, lit a cigarette and called Donny who asked if he could call Cotton back in a few minutes, and he said sure. Cotton's life was about to change and he didn't even know it.

Cotton breezed through a yield sign. The car he pulled out in front of was a police cruiser. The cop hit the blue lights and pulled him over.

After a long wait for his license and proof of insurance to be examined– the officer returned to inform Cotton there were three warrants for his arrest.

"For what?"

"Battery. False imprisonment and preventing a 911 call. Please step out of the car."

Donny called back. The policeman answered Cotton's phone and informed Donny he was headed to the Fulton County Jail.

Turns out on March 25–the day Cotton saw the Snake in the bar with some dude–she went down to the police station that day and filed a false police report against Cotton. The Snake lied in the most heinous fashion. What she did to Cotton–the Snake told the police he did to her. Without any evidence, three warrants were issued for his arrest.

Cotton sat in jail from Monday night until Friday afternoon. He couldn't believe this evil act transpired. How obscene. In jail, his life flashed before his eyes. He thought of his daughter, his parents, his friends, his reputation and his livelihood. Cotton was in serious trouble. A felony charge counted as something one never escaped. The satanic Snake intended to destroy his life.

The nerve-shattering circumstances of being an innocent man accused of crimes he did not commit proved life-altering. Cotton hired a good lawyer, which set him back financially in a way it took years to recover from. His lawyer informed him his options were to stay in jail for two weeks–lose both of his jobs–and wait for his trial date.

Or sign a pre-bond agreement that stated Cotton must attend anger management classes, see a probation officer once a month and have no contact with "the victim". He was fucked either way. That evil cunt. This degrading cycle would continue until Cotton completed the program.

"If you do what I tell you, your record will be expunged when all this is over," Cotton's lawyer told him and he trusted the lawyer. His lawyer also said,

"This woman obviously tried to ruin your life. You're pleading guilty to nothing. You should have pressed charges. But you tried to be nice, and forgot how mentally ill she is, but I hate to tell you, the road to hell is paved with good intentions."

Cotton showed his lawyer every suicidal text, photos of the Snake cutting her wrists, drunken voice messages and her threats she sent to him. For a year, Cotton was treated like a criminal by the system because of the Snake's evil lie. What a nightmare. He was forced to explain to his employers he needed every Tuesday night off to attend his meetings. Cotton counted them out on a calendar.

If he attended one meeting a week he'd be finished in a year. He had to pay for every meeting and every probation visit while losing money at work. If he violated any of the pretrial agreement he went straight to jail. Meanwhile, the Snake ran wild like a famous hooker in the street snorting coke, drinking and sleeping with any man that gave her attention. The satanic circumstances enraged Cotton.

It's difficult to put into words the transformation one undergoes during extreme conditions of a false allegation. Cotton felt serious anxiety. Cotton never heard from the Snake once during this ordeal. He burned anything dealing with her–photos, letters, cards or any item linking them together.

After a nightmarish year, Cotton's record was expunged. His lawyer informed him the DA approached Lily the Snake and informed her Cotton's season in hell expired, and that he refused to plead guilty to her false allegations. They informed the Snake if she were caught in a lie–she would go to jail. Did she want to go to trial? A trial terrified her. The Snake dropped all charges. On Cotton's official expungement document it stated 'State Refuses To Prosecute'.

The legal ordeal ended, but the dark deed still lingered for Cotton. No justice existed for him. A compelling argument could be made that he developed a sort of post stress trauma from this evil woman's lie. The thought of the Snake either enraged or made Cotton sick. He could spot her car a mile away. Few understand what it means to be accused of a crime you did not commit.

It took awhile for Cotton to recover. Six weeks after being exonerated, the Snake called him. The nerve, he thought. Cotton read the text in a New Orleans hotel lobby during a business trip. The Snake wanted to talk. Cotton did not respond. She sent apologetic texts begging him to talk to her. He wanted answers, but it took four months for him to agree to meet the Snake in Piedmont Park.

The Snake apologized, but it sounded insincere as she still grinned that evil smirk of hers. She showed no remorse as if nothing really happened to him. Cotton understood there was no known cure for her madness.

"Never contact me again or I'll get a restraining order," Cotton told her and walked away.

For the next several years, the Snake would call or text him, but he never responded. The Snake used Facebook to get close to his friends. Lily the Snake tried to appear normal as possible to the locals--like any true sociopath. She frequented bars hoping she'd catch a glimpse of Cotton who avoided her favorite taverns. She often approached his friends if they were sitting in a bar.

Around this time, Cotton started dating the beautiful Summer Windsor and he never looked back. Word eventually got back to him that the Snake's three children moved back to Savannah to live with their father because the Snake's sister declared her an unfit mother. That spoke volumes. The Snake attended AA meetings, and made it ninety days sober before she started drinking in bars again, snorting coke and generally making an ass of herself.

Three years later, while still dating Summer, the Snake discovered a new sucker in Rory Davis who proved to be the guy whose name the Snake kept asking Cotton about on The Ides of March, was now her running partner.

Later, Cotton heard the Snake was committed to a nine to twelve month in-house rehabilitation center for women. He also discovered she never explained or admitted to anyone she committed a felony by filing a false police report against him. The Snake lived a lie.

Rehab failed to cure her terminal craziness. The Snake continued operating as a sociopathic alcoholic/drug addict miscreant who fell off the wagon again and tried to be everyone's friend in the community even though she continued snorting powders, drinking and generally running wild like a goat in the street.

As Karma descended her life became dumber and meaner. She slithers through life as a liar of the highest order.

Cotton still remained pissed off at himself for going back to a woman who possessed the remorse of a sociopath and the soul of a prostitute. Lesson learned. He understood the road to hell is paved with good intentions.

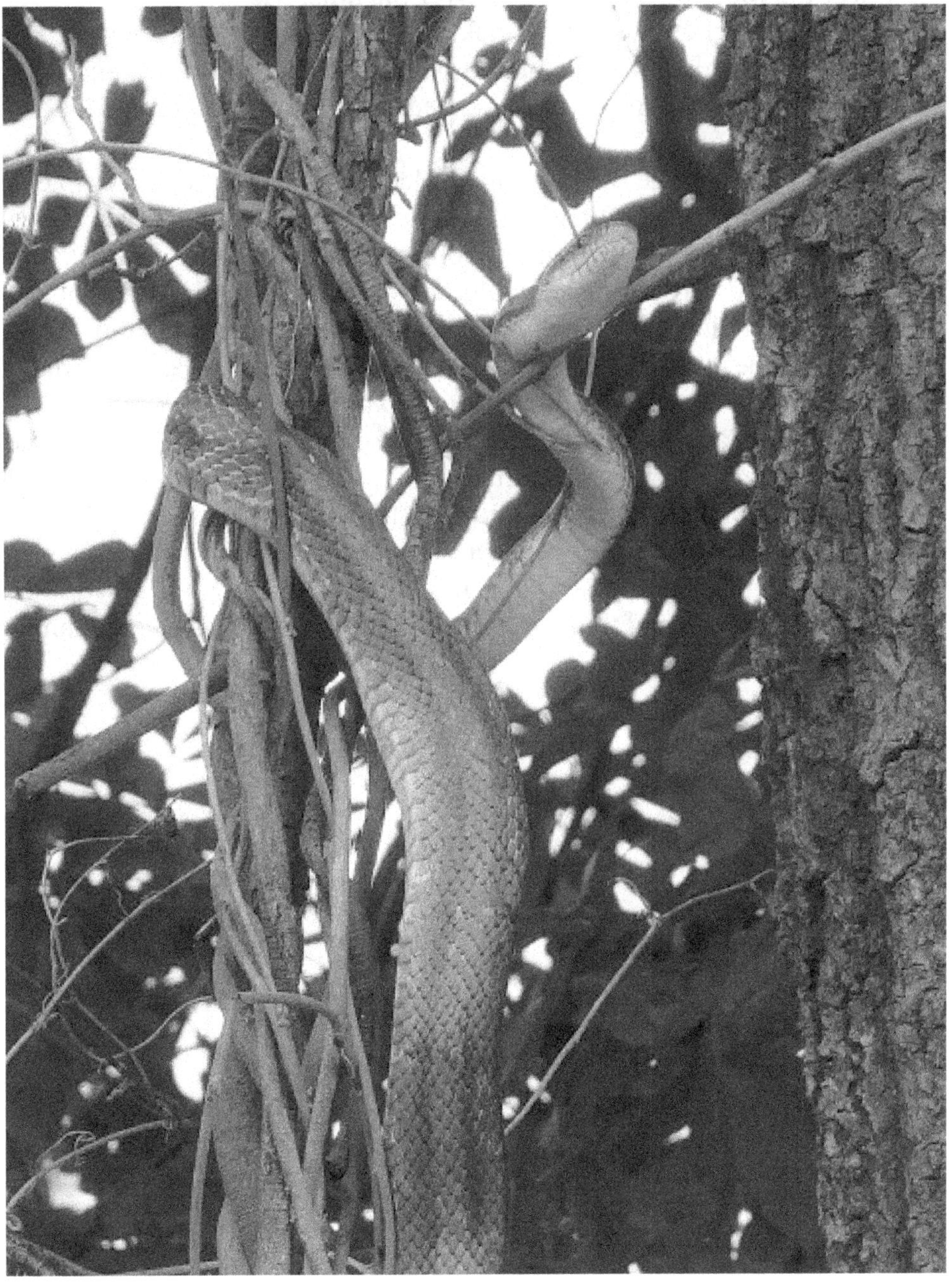

The Four Horsemen

"I hear the four horsemen coming over the hills, friends!"

The street preacher stood on Whitaker Street near Forsyth Park in downtown Savannah as dark storm clouds hovered. People walked by, and most ignored the street preacher. Some glanced at him for only a moment and kept walking.

"The End is near! The world is run on electricity. The Dark Forces intend to disrupt our electricity! What will you do without electricity? Have you saved your souls? Prepare!" Thunder rolled behind the lead colored sky.

His beard appeared long and white. This blue-eyed ranting man looked homeless at first glance. Yet, he seemed clean, ageless and unearthly.

"These are the end times! It's not a question if the grid will go, but when! Plagues and pestilence will soon arrive! Prepare!"

The street preacher never remained in the same location. Every day he preached from a different street corner.

"The Dark Forces will target Electricity! You got Russian and Chinese warships off our coast! They want a New World Order! You can't stop what's coming! Pray to Jesus! That's all you can do!"

Rain began to fall, and thunder rumbled again in the distance like familiar hoofprints.

83

Crossroads

"I went to the crossroad, fell down on my knees."
--Robert Johnson

Mack Sweetblood watched the summer rain evaporate in a festering heat. The phone never rang less these days. Surrounded by imitators, he realized, at this point, most of the local artists only copied his work. However, when they needed his professional expertise they campaigned for his help. When the shoe was on the other foot they were nowhere to be found.

One formidable media outlet used an old magazine's model–which Sweetblood helped create–and augmented it as their own once his employer's magazine went under. Locals enjoyed watching him struggle. They received him with indifference at best.

The cell phone hurt photography for professionals. These copycats sniffed out his work like hellhounds and within a month they'd travel to the same place and take a photograph from the same perspective. He also felt their jealousy regarding his artistic connections. Two years passed since Sweetblood worked a good paying assignment.

When acclaimed artists vouched for his work these locals acted like they always were the first to arrive at the dance. But, they bought nothing. He competed with artists of the highest order, while people with cell phones fancied themselves stars. The prophet hath no honor in thy homeland. His competition watched him closely. A mean-spirited intention hounded Sweetblood.

God forbid, he succeed without them. For years, he wondered if it were intentional neglect but he couldn't confirm his gut instinct until he had work to sell. Meanwhile, the self-proclaimed champions of the arts never contributed to his cause even though they burned money on far less important matters or artists.

He waited. He understood he possessed something they didn't, and that was talent. He endured the Johnny-Come-Latelys and the snarky millennial social media hot shots parading themselves with the moxie of dumb roosters.

Sweetblood also dealt with a local literary tourist who started taking pictures of the same subject matter. A 62-year old car salesman retires. Two years later, he decides he's a poet. He strongarms an editor into publishing some of his half-baked poems. Consequently, on social media he becomes a self-absorbed, narcissistic, self-appointed Poet Laureate. He spouts psychobabble on social media, earns some 'likes'–and thinks his work is Art.

Yet, no one has the heart to tell him his poetry sucks. A self-promoter of the highest order...

The literary tourist's modus operandi is to ride the coattails of his talented friends to promote his own work instead of learning how to write. Unfortunately, hustling cars is not the same as hustling poetry. He believes if he keeps the right company he'll be a star or if he brags about himself enough he will convince civilians he's the 'real deal'. His inflated sense of talent proved unfounded.

Four years ago, the literary tourist was selling used Buicks and now he's a songwriter, writer and poet on par with, in his own words, "T.S. Eliot." Yet, he imitates and steals what he can and calls it his own. He doesn't know roads are paved with the bones of literary tourists. In person, he talks at you,

"Yeah, just send me your email connections," then he disconnects the call.

The literary tourist's work proved derivative. Nothing revelatory. He wrote on Facebook that his poems stood as prophetic. And nine times out of ten the story has been written many times and each version proves stronger than his. So, Sweetblood avoided such pretenders like the literary tourist and they disliked him for his distance.

And then the life-changing call came.

"Maybe you should cut a deal, Sweetblood. Your work will sell if you do."

"I'm not making a deal with you."

"I don't see any other choice."

"There's always a choice. No deal."

"Consider it. We both know you're not very employable at anything other than your talents. And big players will sell your work. I'll be in touch..."

Sweetblood's ulcer burned. The July morning sun sliced through the blinds. A behavior sink racked his body, and soul. Depression. How could his only alternative be making a deal with the Devil?

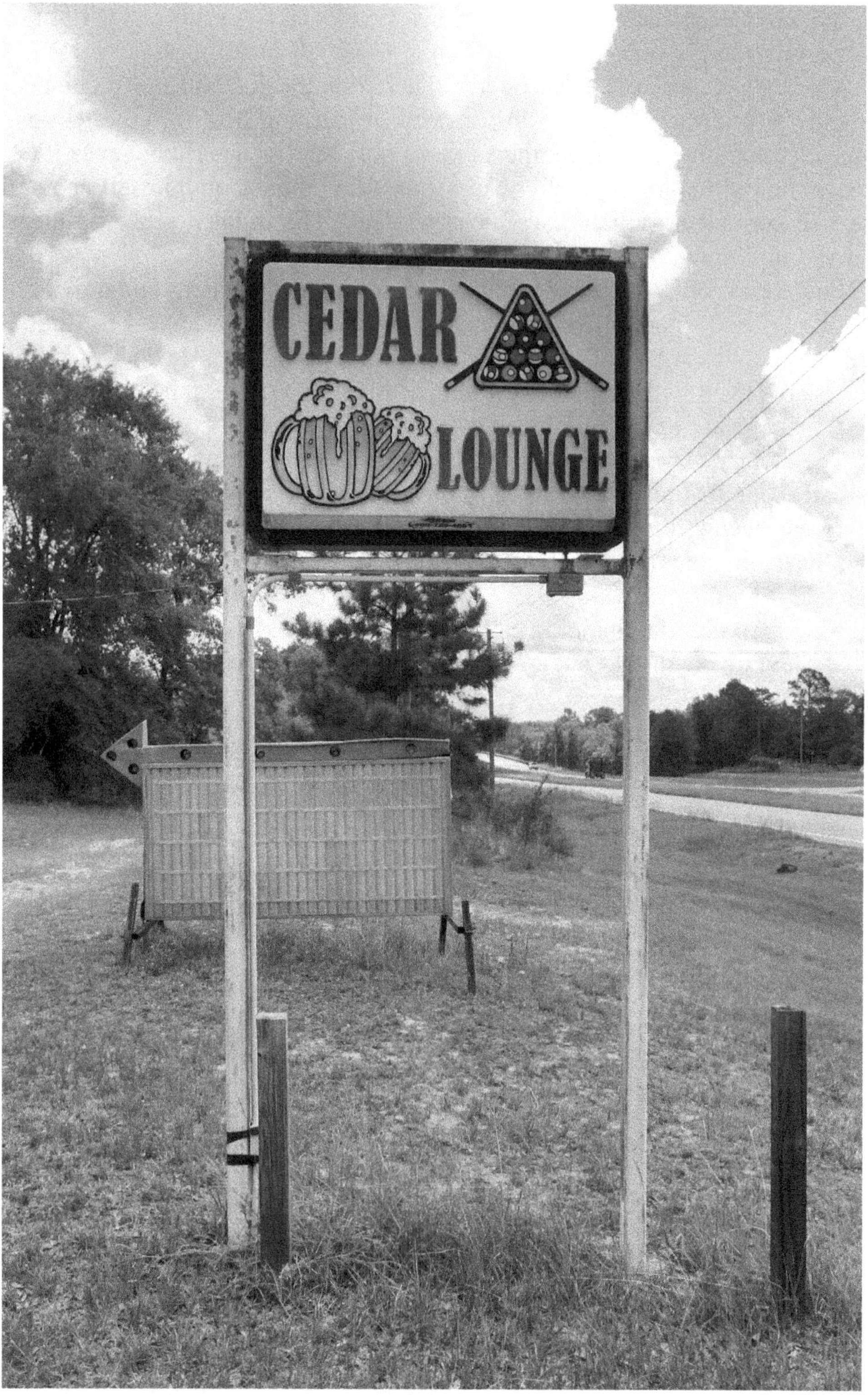
CEDAR
LOUNGE

Power Grid Blues

"I'm tired of Darkness."

"It goes to show how modern civilization crumbles in three days without electricity."

"No ATMs. No gas. No food. No water. No internet. No lights. Pandemonium. Back to the stone ages in two weeks. It started with that virus."

"This shit is Biblical. Apocalyptic. Death is all around."

"After three weeks–it's all gangs. Looting. I hear disease is spreading due to lack of sanitation. Back to the Stone Age..."

"The stench is nauseating."

"America is now a war zone. History told us this would happen. But a pampered and decadent society proves shortsighted."

"How long will we stay here?"

"Until we're safe enough to leave this camp and escape to the coast."

Dear Ella

Dear Ella,

Somehow I always knew it would come to this. I always worried about being in the exact position I face now. My worst fears became realities. Since time is short I just wanted to say a few things I want you to carry with you everywhere you go. I wanted to write it for your keepsake. I tell you all this anyway, but the written word lasts.

I love you. I will always love you. I've never loved anyone like I've loved you. I'm not perfect, and I made mistakes. I look back--and two or three bad decisions altered the course of my entire life. Ultimately, my poor decisions affected us at certain times--and I know it. I will take them to my grave. But, I always loved you more than anything--even at my lowest ebb. You were my crown jewel. It will remain that way even when I'm gone.

I thought I'd have more time. But, life doesn't work that way. I've taken care of business matters. I'm leaving everything to you. Everything is in order. My lawyer's name is John Martin. I've enclosed his number. Maybe some of those things will remind you of me. And your grandparents. I hope I've never been an embarrassment to you. Or if I have been, I'm sorry and it was never my intention. I hope all this doesn't make you upset with me. I'm sorry for any inconvenience, pain or anger.

I feel like I let you down. I wish we could've spent more time together. I'm so sorry. I guess I should've gone to the doctor earlier. Money for insurance was always a hassle in our country's state of affairs--especially for me, but the Lord dictates our time.

I always wondered that when you die if God allows you to go help people you love. I'm sure he does, and I'll always be with you and help you.

You are a brilliant, beautiful and soulful young lady. The world is a mean place. Always trust yourself. Trust God. Be good as you can. I know you will. I just wish I could be around to see all the great things you'll do. I always missed you. I'll always be with you. And when you feel sad, just remember the good times, our laughs and look at all our pictures. It was all real.

I love you more than words can tell. Always will.

                      Love,
                      Dad

The Grand Princess

"I told Delia I had a bad feeling about this trip as soon as we stepped on the ship," he told his father from the small cabin.

"I guess you never thought a romantic cruise to Hawaii on the Grand Princess would turn into this debacle."

"It's a fucking nightmare. I'm never getting on a cruise ship again."

"The news is saying 21 passengers and crew on your boat are infected with this damn Coronavirus. So, you're docking in Oakland?"

"Yeah. They don't tell us much. We're all stuck in our rooms watching the same news you are. We're just watching TV, checking our phones and looking at the news in this tiny cabin with no windows. I heard those of us from Georgia will be taken to Dobbins Air Force base to get tested and quarantined."

"How do you feel?"

"I feel okay. Delia is not feeling so hot–but it's hard not to feel weird. It's a combination of paranoia, fear and hypochondria. We have a dead guy on the boat from this virus, and it's not a good feeling. We don't have windows.

"I hear people are freaking out. Running out of their medications. The crew is handing out crafts like crossword puzzles and jewelry kits to keep people from going totally insane. The halls are empty, it's creepy."

"Well, all you can do is what they tell you. How are they handling the food?"

"Actually, the food isn't bad. Under normal circumstances it would be great–lobster, burgers and everything we paid for on this godforsaken trip. But you worry if the food was handled by an infected person somewhere, so I've not been really hungry. Each day they give us a sheet to fill out with our meal choices. They bring the food right to the room. All events on the boat are cancelled. They let you know when you are allowed to get fresh air. Delia mentioned a few days ago how people were coughing and hacking all around us. She's not amused."

"I sure as hell hope they refund the money."

"Oh, she will see to that one."

"Well, this virus looks serious. I heard a doctor say we should stock up on groceries for three months. I mean who knows who's infected. Italy is shut down basically. Everyday the numbers go up. And the Chinese are not telling us how bad it is there, I don't think. They say the Chinese are burning hundreds of dead bodies. It's hard to know what to believe. We have a pandemic on our hands. Shit, it could hit the homeless. Airports. Subways. Jesus."

"Yeah, shit like this alters history. How's Mom?"

"Stubborn as ever. Your mother said Target is out of hand sanitizer already. I told her she couldn't go to church or the hospital to visit Hazel with her weak lungs and she got pissed. But I think she's starting to get with the program. But she cringes at the thought of me grocery shopping. But, it could get worse. I'm just worried about y'all getting off that boat."

"Oh, let me tell you. Tell Mom to take it easy. Well, I'll let you go for now. We love y'all."

"We love you too."

"I'll call you when we get an update."

"Okay son, everything is going to be okay."

"We shall see."

OKEFENOKEE
CITY
LIMITS
CAUTION
ALLIGATOR
CROSSING
NEXT
3 MILES

UFOs Over The Okefenokee Swamp

Located sixty miles from the Georgia coast, the Okefenokee Swamp covers over almost five-hundred thousand acres. The Okefenokee leads to the Gulf of Mexico. The Native Americans such as Creek and Seminole Indians inhabited the swamp. This magical place earned the name "Land of the Trembling Earth". The Okefenokee retains a spooky, mysterious vibration. The vast black water, beautiful cypress groves, Spanish moss, water lilies, exaggerated reflections and a loss of any sense of direction contribute to its timeless mystery.

Alligators, poisonous snakes and even meat eating plants (hooded pitchers eat insects) live in the Swamp. Over six-hundred species of plants, twenty species of snakes, thirty-nine kinds of fish and over two-hundred kinds of birds thrive in the Okefenokee. Even black bears. The Swamp's biodiversity ranks among the highest on the planet.

On the north edge of the Okefenokee is a town called Waycross, Georgia. I first visited the Okefenokee in 1974. The Wildlife Refuge headquarters are located in Folkston, GA.

For centuries, strange stories emerged from the Okefenokee Swamp such as UFO sightings, Pig Man, curses, abductions and Native American ghost stories. One could write a book regarding all the strange occurrences that transpired in the Land of the Trembling Earth.

The Okefenokee Wildlife Refuge serves as a source and depot for swamp visitors. Ware County, Georgia, operated in the turpentine and lumber business during the 19th century. The place looks exactly like it did two thousand years ago.

In 1937, the Okefenokee became "protected from progress".

I'll not submit specific years or previous strange occurrences because you can look it all up on the Internet, but I want to give you some background information before we get to this story.

A former Everglades National Park ranger went missing for forty days in the Okefenokee. Some speculation indicated an alien abduction was possible, but the ranger never admitted what actually happened. Two years later, a local newspaper reported a "shiny object" flying in the sky over the Okefenokee.

Swamp gas exists as an explanation of decaying plants and peat beneath the water that creates a gas, which becomes a luminescence called "foxfire". These flashes have been reported to chase folks. Sometimes the swamp is burned in systematic places for the overall health of the land and to control future forest fires.

There's no commercial nonsense in the Swamp. All tours remain guided by the state. It's no place for an outsider to get lost. And you certainly run the risk of running up on a pissed off female gator if you're near her babies. Any number of perilous unforeseen situations may arise.

II

On a risky research trip, I decided to revisit the Swamp several years ago. I'd been there many times since 1974, but this visit proved different. This time I planned to spend the night, but no unofficial overnight camping is allowed in the Swamp. So, I contacted the most adept outdoorsman I'd ever known, Paul Stevens. Convincing him to undertake such a strange request required two days worth of me explaining my intention, which was to capture something on film out of the ordinary. Paul reluctantly agreed since he heard of strange activity in the area as well. He also existed as an adventurer of the highest order, and remained unfazed by moderate risk.

Three days later our friend Zeke dropped us off, and we put kayaks in at the Suwannee Canal by Folkston, Georgia, instead of the official Stephen Foster entry.

Dust of rumor circulated Twin Pines Minerals intended to start mining the swamp soon. DuPont abandoned their plant in the swamp causing leakage in neighboring towns, which some say led to one of the highest cancer rates in children across the country.

"There's no good reception here," Paul said as we pulled the kayaks up on Billy's Island, near Fargo, Georgia, a couple of hours later. I kept thinking about the park ranger that was lost out here for forty days. I did not mention the story to Paul.

In the early 1900s, a logging camp operated on Billy's Island. Remnants of the old timber business remain on the island such as tree-clearing machines. An entire community lived here in those days with grocery stores and even a movie theatre. Bootleggers ran their moonshine business from the depths of these rare environs. An ancient Indian mound also exists on the island that dates back to 500 AD. Rare earth, indeed.

"This is a pretty good spot. Gators aren't aggressive at this time of year. And no fires because if anyone catches us out here it will be a Federal issue."

It was a late afternoon in early December. The peaceful, surrounding beauty proved awe inspiring. An egret disappeared into the shadows. But I wondered how the mood would change late at night when weird nocturnal vibrations descended. It reminded me of how dependent we are on technology. How useful it can be–but we're the first generation to attempt using GPS in the Okefenokee. Technology serves no real purpose in the Okefenokee.

In every direction the swamp looked the same. Weird reflections cast strange images on the dark water. Navigating at night in any direction would prove unwise. Few folks traveled back this far in the Swamp. I noticed a female barred owl in a tree looking down at us. Natural wonders exist in every direction.

Only a fool would assume they are in control in the Okefenokee Swamp. This is the great unknown. I tried to send out positive waves to the land projecting peace as we paddled on the way in. I think it was my fascination with the concept of time travel. Hell, this could be the heart of darkness for all I knew. A gator watched us paddle by from afar.

We assembled our separate tents, ate some beef jerky and drank bottled water. Strange sounds could be heard as the sun set. I experienced an eerie feeling like we were being watched, but not by humans. An unease gripped me.

I stared up at the stars. An old spirit seemed to sway in the chilly breeze. Paul retired to his tent first. I looked for anything out of the ordinary. Even President Jimmy Carter filled out an official report with the International UFO Bureau in Oklahoma City regarding a UFO experience Carter witnessed in Leary, Georgia, during 1969. Leary is about two and a half hours from here. Yet, Georgia does not rank high on the list of states with real high UFO sightings. But, I'd heard from a family friend that recent activity existed near the swamp.

Maybe we'd stay two nights. Finally, around 3am I climbed into my tent.

At 3:37am a strange light flashed in the sky and awoke me from a light sleep.

"Paul?"

He did not answer. I crawled out of my tent. I noticed his tent was open and he was not in it. Another weird flash appeared in the sky and then sudden darkness.

"Paul!?"

Nothing. He vanished. I panicked. I called out to him again. I realized that my "research trip" perhaps just turned ugly. I used my flashlight to scan the perimeter. Total silence surrounded me. The sudden silence continued for hours it seemed. No creature made a sound. No phone reception existed to call Paul's phone. I told myself maybe he took a walk.

At sunrise, I felt hesitant to kayak anywhere and run the risk of getting lost. And I could not leave without him. How would I explain his disappearance? I knew the rest of my life was at stake. Fuck. Paul, the most adept outdoorsman I knew, disappeared in the Okefenokee Swamp, and we were technically trespassing.

I didn't want to call out too many times fearing I may attract some sort of unwanted attention–by anyone or anything. I decided to wait it out. It was at least five miles back to our point of entry. And GPS on my phone proved useless. I wasn't sure I could navigate my way out of the swamp at this hour for help anyway. I paced all day in distress.

After another sleepless night, around noon, just before I was about to paddle out in sheer desperation and get help because my phone battery was dying, I heard movement in the water. I expected an alligator or some agent of darkness. Then I watched a disheveled-looking Paul appear out of a nearby Cypress grove, wading in knee-deep water back to our camp.

"Holy fuck, man! Where have you been?"

"I don't know. How long have I been gone?"

"Two days. I thought you got eaten by a gator or snake-bit." I gave him a hug.

"I don't remember anything except a bright light hovering over me. And now I have this weird triangle looking mark on my left hand that hurts if I touch it."

I'd never seen such a thing. It made my skin crawl.

"We gotta get out of here."

"There are UFOs over the Okefenokee. Never tell anyone about this trip," he said.

"Are you okay?"

"We need to get back."

We paddled the kayaks back to Folkston without speaking. We never mentioned the Okefenokee again. In fact, Paul kept a very low profile from that day on. A year later, he sold his lucrative fishing charter business, moved to Atlanta and never returned to the Land of the Trembling Earth.

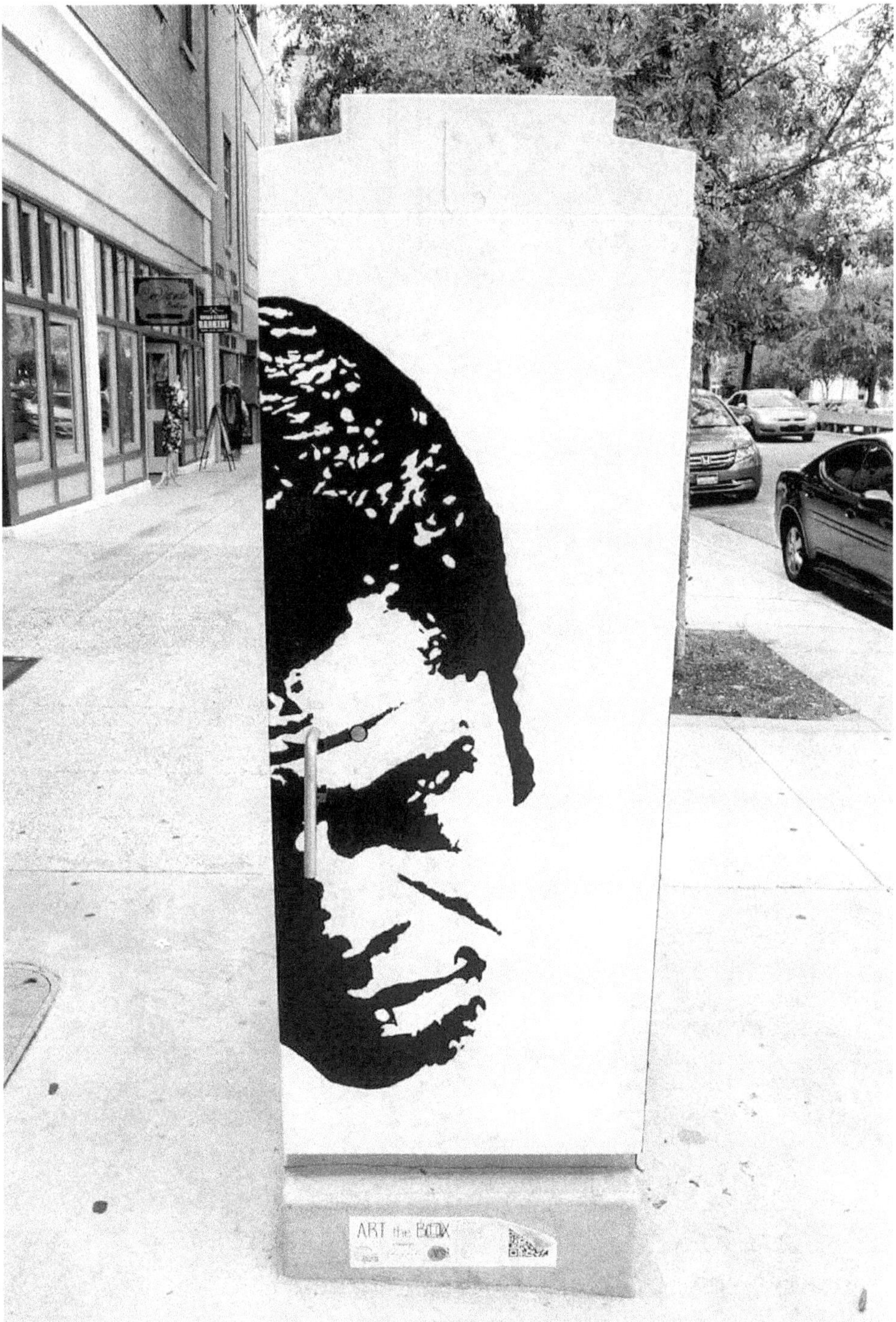
ART the BOX

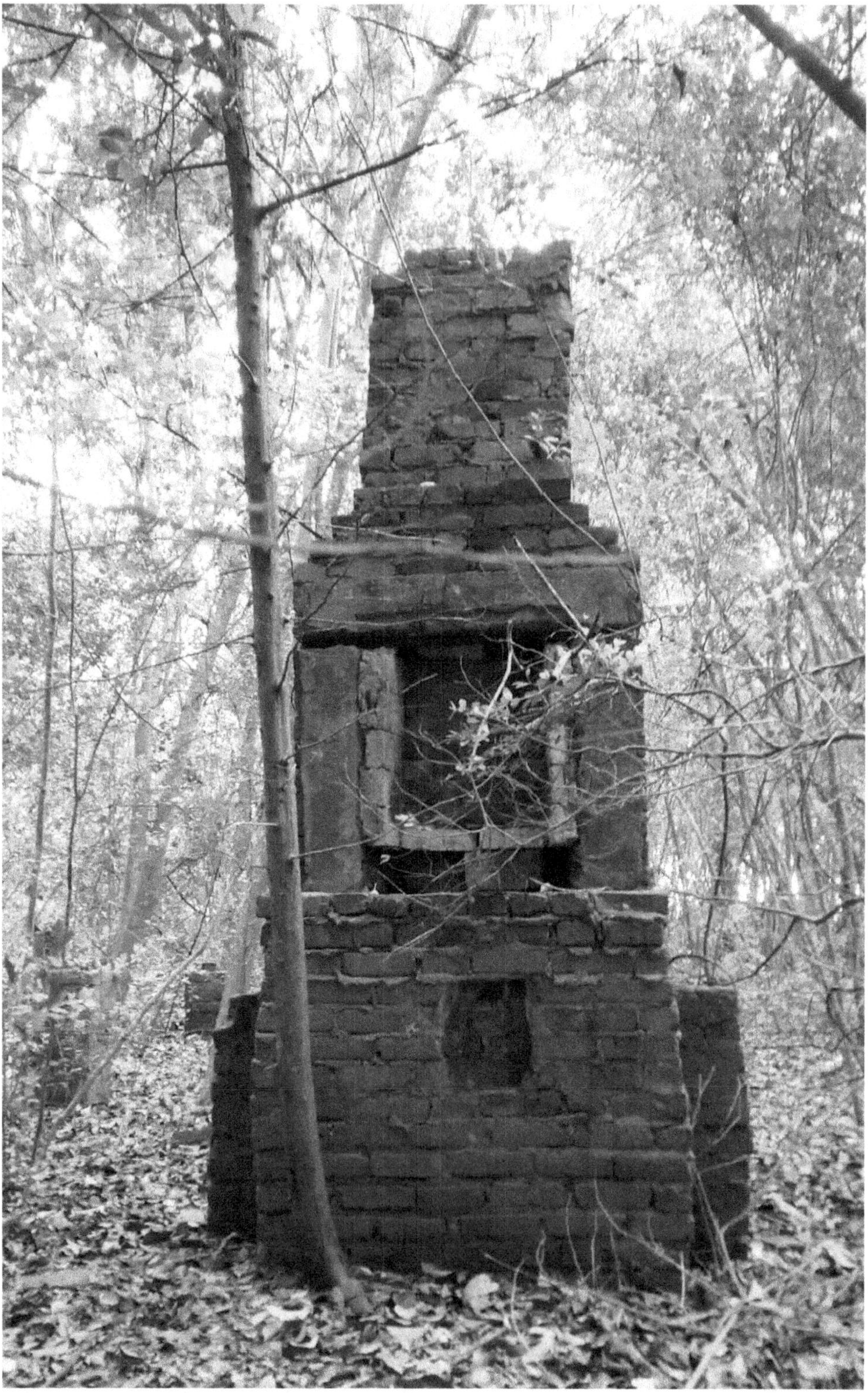

99